THE SECRETS OF
CEDAR FARM

CARISSA ANN LYNCH

One More Chapter
a division of HarperCollins*Publishers*
1 London Bridge Street
London SE1 9GF
www.harpercollins.co.uk
HarperCollins*Publishers*
1st Floor, Watermarque Building, Ringsend Road
Dublin 4, Ireland

This paperback edition 2022
First published in Great Britain in ebook format
by HarperCollins*Publishers* 2022
Copyright © Carissa Ann Lynch 2022
Carissa Ann Lynch asserts the moral right to be identified
as the author of this work

A catalogue record of this book is available from the British Library

ISBN: 978-0-00-852030-4

Carissa Ann Lynch is a *USA Today*-bestselling author. She resides in Floyds Knobs, Indiana with her husband, children, and collection of books. She's always loved to read and never considered herself a "writer" until a few years ago when she couldn't find a book to read and decided to try writing her own story. With a background in psychology, she's always been a little obsessed with the darker areas of the mind and social problems.

carissaannlynch.wordpress.com

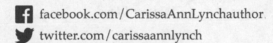 facebook.com/CarissaAnnLynchauthor
twitter.com/carissaannlynch

Also by Carissa Ann Lynch

Adversity truly introduces us to ourselves.
Alcoholics Anonymous, The Big Book, page 530

To Chelsi—thank you for the books, the laughs, and the late-night inspiration.

Introduction

Behind every family is a story. Within that story, there's always someone like me.

The black sheep. The troubled one. Resident fuck-up. Whatever you want to call it… that's me.

Sometimes the title is well-earned—we're outsiders because we deserve to be. Other times, it's for one reason and one reason only—we know too much.

Banish the person, banish the secrets…

Chapter One

STEP 1: HONESTY

"**Y**ou look too young to be a widow."

It wasn't the first time I'd heard those words.

Not the first time I'd told this lie: "He died in battle."

It's a quick way to shut down questions because—let's face it—twenty-four is too young to lose your spouse, and, this way, everyone assumes he died valiantly on the battlefield, fighting whoever the powers that be designated as the current bad guy.

I tried to imagine Finn as a Viking, disgruntled and daring. His lips curled at the corners, a secret smile. *We used to share so many of those.*

"I'm sorry for your loss. Which branch did he serve in?"

Empathetic brown eyes rose to meet mine, the cab driver watching in the rearview mirror. He was handsome, fortyish. Kind. Perhaps big and strong, too, but nothing compared to my fantasy of Finn the Viking.

I sighed, the rush of breath louder than I'd intended.

This entire conversation was my fault, for correcting the driver when he referred to me as "Miss Campbell" at pick-up. It was *Mrs.* At least it should have been...

I looked out the window, glaring at the blurry rows of soybean and corn, imagining Finn's feathery lashes, the rough pads of his thumbs... and *that* laugh, the kind that requires you to laugh with your whole chest when you do it. God, how I loved his laugh.

Viking, he was not. But, oh how he made me smile...

Hmm... which branch did he serve in?

"Not the kind with medals and flags," I said, finally.

The marriage part was a lie too—like so many things that happened between us, I was stretching the truth.

Finn and I were engaged, not married yet, when it happened. We said we were married so often that perhaps we even believed it.

But then Finn died. And our plans, our dreams... they all died with him in the middle of our junky living-room floor on a cold winter night. Our junky house and our junkie ways... His death was as inevitable as me landing here, in rural Indiana, forced to grovel with an aunt and uncle I barely knew.

Give my daughter back. PLEASE.

The driver must not have heard me, because next thing I knew, he was talking about his own father, an accomplished military pilot...

Finn died in battle.

It was *sort of* a lie. Though not really.

Finn was never a soldier, but he did, in fact, wage war.

2

Battling his demons, putting his body through hell in its war with opioid addiction, until his body finally threw out the white flag of defeat…

You won, Finn. Your destructive willpower outlasted the shell you were born in, just like you always said it would. And now, you'll never get the chance to make me smile or laugh again…

No more secret smiles for me.

The rest of the cab ride was silent, much to my relief.

My hands shook as I remembered the letter in my hands: the last (and only) letter Gemma wrote me while I was gone in rehab. But did two sentences really count as a letter?

I miss you. I hate it here Mom.

Those words, as much as it pained me to read them, gave me one small glimmer of hope—*Gemma still calls me Mom.*

Not her deadbeat father, not my eccentric aunt and uncle… not my catty never-became-my-sister-in-law Jewel.

Me.

I'm Mom. And, regardless of my past mistakes, I always will be.

The driver followed a snaky paved road, past a meadow teeming with wildflowers. Rolling my window down, I drew in the heady perfume.

Nice to catch a break from the cornfields and cattle shit.

A gentle hill arose from the earth, and then the cab rattled to a stop.

"Here we are, Ma'am," the driver said, careful not to call me "Miss" again.

After hours of passing nothing but grainy farmland, smudgy patches of churches and painted farmhouses... I was finally here.

The rotting monstrosity rose before me, like a bad dream. I lowered my sunglasses, taking it all in.

The house had been beautiful once, you could tell. But the rotten, peeling Victorian that belonged to my aunt and uncle looked to be on the verge of collapse. Steeply pitched points and arched windows gave the house a gothic appeal.

Creepy.

Now this is my daughter's home, too, I thought, unable to hide my shock and dismay.

Truth was, I could barely remember Cedar Farm from my youth, having spent so little time here. In my mind's eye, I'd imagined a cutesy farmhouse, something wholesome with chickens and ducks. Not this dilapidated, pseudo-haunted house.

But it was my aunt and uncle who had turned up at my court hearing after Finn's overdose and my third arrest. It was they who had volunteered to take custody so that Gemma didn't become a ward of the state. With my own parents dead and gone, the chances of finding an alternative to foster care had seemed slim... until my long-lost relatives showed up to save the day.

Deep down, I knew I should feel more grateful toward Sara and Francis. They had taken in my daughter, whom they had never met… and now they were offering to take me too.

You can stay with us until you're ready to bring her home, Aunt Sara had offered over the phone when I was fresh out of rehab.

But coming here, after ninety days of treatment and feeling disconnected from my daughter, all I could feel was bottled-up fear. Fear that they wouldn't give her back. Fear that she wouldn't remember how close we once were… Only seven, Gemma's resilient heart and mind might help her block me out for good…

I'm clean. I'm sober. I'm taking my meds. I'm working the program. But good luck convincing the judge of that.

And this house… It was nothing at all like what I expected. Not where I would have wanted to leave my daughter. But in times of desperation, I couldn't afford to be picky, could I? And, after all, it was my own fault she'd had to come here.

I have to accept the blame for putting her in this position to begin with.

The driver popped the trunk and handed me the skinny yellow suitcase I'd had since I was a teenager. It contained extraordinarily little—five outfits, some panties and socks, a few toiletries, and my AA bible, also known as the *Big Book*.

"Thank you, sir."

I'd paid the driver in advance online, but I knew I should offer a tip. I scrounged through my dress pockets for a five and two ones, guiltily handing over what little loose cash I had.

The driver, in a strange old-fashioned gesture, tipped his hat and took a bow before climbing back behind the wheel. Gravel dust tickled my nose and throat as he rumbled away, leaving me here alone in front of the crumbling house holding the few possessions I owned. The only thing I cared about was inside that house, my sweet daughter…

A tire swing moved back and forth, creaking in the wind. I waited for the screen door to pop open, my aunt and uncle, or (hopefully) Gemma, to emerge to greet me. But nobody came. The grumbling of tires disappeared in the distance, and suddenly, I felt very alone.

I looked left then right, taking in the vast open cornfields on either side of the house and the hulking shadow of trees beyond it… There wasn't a neighbor around for miles, I realized.

The house looked even more dilapidated as I approached, the eyes of two ghastly stone creatures leering down at me from above. This was the first time I'd seen a gargoyle in real life. It reminded me of old vampire movies, and I shivered. The home was large and historic, Victorian according to Aunt Sara, but the gargoyles seemed over the top. I tried to recall what I knew about gargoyles… *Aren't they supposed to ward off evil or something? Maybe that's not such a bad thing after all I've gone through this year,* I considered.

Although I should have remembered the house from my childhood, nothing about this place felt familiar.

I'd been younger than Gemma when Mom and I had come to visit her sister Sara.

Nothing about this place felt like it should. Most of all, my aunt and uncle themselves were complete strangers to me. I didn't even know who they were at first when they showed up in court. As grateful as I was for their help, it seemed obvious that my daughter wasn't happy here. Her recent, snappy letter proved that as much.

I'd mailed out dozens of letters, all of which had gone unanswered until I'd received her short reply.

Considering how eerie and isolated it is out here, I can see why she hates it. This isn't at all what I expected. What other surprises are in store for me? I wondered, overcome with a sense of foreboding.

Steadily, I gripped my suitcase and approached the house.

I must get my daughter back, at all costs, and take her home to Chicago.

Chapter Two

The house looked out of place: this dark Victorian monster in the middle of a desolated cornfield... almost like it had been picked up from some ancient era and dropped from the heavens above. I couldn't shake the thought that it didn't belong. But who was I kidding? *I don't belong here, either. And neither does my daughter.*

The once-white paint was peeling now, and I fought the urge to pluck a strip and peel it all the way back as I rapped my knuckles on the old screen door.

Breathless, I held on to my suitcase, fingers white and achy with nerves. I waited. Then waited some more. A flutter of excitement at seeing Gemma and anxiety at facing my relatives raced through me, making my stomach twist and curl noisily as the minutes ticked by. Like an obscene version of "the butterflies" I couldn't get rid of... For a moment, I almost wished I'd taken an extra dose of my anti-anxiety medication on the way here. But the doctor's voice reverberated in my head: *It's important that you take your meds as prescribed. Even though these are non-narcotic, make sure you follow the dose and don't over-medicate.*

I drummed my fingers on the screen door, waiting.

When no one came, that flutter turned to something else —*what if I've come to the wrong place? What if I'm stuck out here, this house straight out of the* Texas Chainsaw Massacre *movie, with no ride to get me back into town? Where is Gemma?*

I moved to the dusty front window and cupped my hands around my face, squinting to see in.

There was no one inside as far as I could tell, but I was relieved to see the house was better kept on the inside than the out, and there were no chainsaw-wielding weirdos.

Through the window, I could see a lavish room with Oriental rugs and the kind of furniture you'd read about in a novel, timeless and Dickensian. There was an ornate fireplace and thick wooden shelves lined with books.

The opposite of our shabby little apartment in Illinois. Six hundred square feet, the apartment had only one door in the entire unit—the arched entrance to the bathroom, that separated it from the kitchen/living room/bedroom that bled together like a heaping tumor. As much as I complained about the lack of space and storage, I wouldn't have traded our compact place in the city for anywhere else.

Certainly not a place like this, I thought, returning to the yard to look up at the second-floor windows. The gargoyles stared back at me, eyes dark and accusatory. They were perched for flight, as though any minute now they might break free from their stony restraints.

I returned to the front door, knocking harder this time; then, finally, I left my suitcase on the porch and wove my way around the back of the property.

It was here that I caught my first glimpse of the past— the Belladonna statue, mother and daughter, and the crumbling fountain and koi pond I recognized from my childhood. In a trance, I walked straight toward one of the statues. It was streaked with lichen and crumbling, little pieces of marble clinging to the soles of my thrift-store sneakers. For a moment, I was a child again... Mom and I, racing through the yard, ducking behind statues, hair floating like kites in the wind as we played a game I liked to call "Palace Garden".

I couldn't believe I'd forgotten until now... How old must I have been, three or four...?

Yes, I have been here before.

I can't remember the inside of the house, but I remember these mysterious grounds ... the secrets I thought they might hold...

How strange it is that those slivers of memory come floating back in an instant, catching us by surprise...

"Norah, dear! Is that you?"

I jumped at the sound of a woman's voice, pulling my hand away from the broken, weathered nose of a sweet cherub. I hadn't heard anyone pull up, only the gentle breeze whistling between the statues, through the poorly trimmed hedges and trees. *The garden and lands were always wild. But not this rundown. Not this unkempt,* I remembered.

When I turned around at the sound of her voice, it took me a moment to recognize her.

Sara looked like an older version of my mother, but frailer. People often said my mother had reminded them of a young Meryl Streep. I didn't see it.

Aunt Sara had long gray hair that trailed all the way down her back. But those soft green eyes that matched my mother's were patient and kind; she had that lit-from-within glow I recognized and remembered, from somewhere dark and dusty in my brain...

That day in court when she'd shown up like my last saving grace in a moment of desperation—I'd never forget it. Her eyes, so much like my mother's, had given me a small sense of ease.

"It's me. So nice to see you again, Aunt Sara." Like the driver, I felt a strange urge to take a bow or offer a curtsy. She was wearing a thin white dress and leather sandals, perfectly matched for the sticky heat of early August.

"Come here, little one."

Sara opened her arms and, surprising myself, I let her wrap me into a tight hug. It had been so long since I'd touched another person; there were strict no-contact rules in rehab between patients and staff, as well as between residents.

Aunt Sara felt light and bony in my arms, and for a moment, it reminded me... it reminded me of Finn at the end, when he lost so much weight because of the drugs. *His collarbones sharp as daggers, his once soft belly concave. Ripples of his rib bones poking me through the sheets...*

Shivering, I stepped back from my aunt and grimaced as

12

I shook off memories of Finn's final days. "Where's Gemma?"

A strange look flickered over Sara's face, but, in a flash, it was gone. She smiled, her big perfect teeth reminding me of my mother again.

"We just got back from having ice-cream in town. I had no idea you'd be here so early."

I glanced at my watch. It was nearly five, making me a half hour late. For a moment, I wondered if we were in different time zones and I'd made a mistake... *I'll have to check the clocks inside later, adjust my watch,* I decided.

I looked around the yard, and behind Sara, eager to see my daughter. Ninety days isn't that long, but it's an eternity when it comes to the ones you love. And, in those long months, I knew a lot could change with a seven-year-old.

"Oh, she's gone inside with Francis and little Susie. They went through the front door. They're so hyper from all the sugar and excited about their playdate."

Playdate?

"Aww, how sweet," I murmured. I'd waited so long to see Gemma; I couldn't wait a second more. I started walking toward the front of the house and Sara fell in step beside me.

"Susie is Merrill's daughter," she explained. "They're close to the same age. I thought it would be nice for Gemma to make a few family friends while she's here."

"How nice," I said. "Who's Merrill again?"

"Ah. Francis's sister. My sister-in-law. You're going to love her, I promise."

"I'm sure I will," I said, trying to hide my discomfort at the thought of sticking around long enough to get to know Francis's family. The last thing I wanted to do was try to make a long-lost connection with extended family...

Sara was my mother's sister; although I'd met her husband Francis when I was little, too, I knew very little about the man. When my mother mentioned her sister in the past—which wasn't often—she rarely brought up her husband. And I didn't remember meeting him as a child, either, most of my memories from that time smudgy or non-existent...

The last time I saw them was my mother's funeral, I realized. As though becoming a young single mother wasn't hard enough, I'd lost my own mother to cancer before the age of twenty. I wasn't used to having family support, so this whole arrangement felt beyond strange. Now, being here and seeing the creepy house and the crumbling grounds, the whole thing felt even stranger.

As we stepped over the threshold, Sara carrying my suitcase despite my protests, I took a deep breath. I was so happy to see my daughter again, but also jittery and nervous, adrenaline running through me like a live wire.

"They already went upstairs," came a gruff voice from somewhere deeper in the house.

"Francis, come see your niece," Sara scolded, motioning for me to take a seat on an uncomfortable-looking red velvet chaise lounge. Floor-to-ceiling shelves lined the walls, filled with dog-eared paperbacks, hardcover classics, and an odd assortment of knick-knacks clogging every open nook and space. I met the glassy eyes of a dusty porcelain doll, eyes then drifting to a bizarre line of oil paintings on the wall.

There was a tug of recognition… a flutter of something remembered, then lost.

The room had a dampness to it, triggering another memory… one that was so fleeting I couldn't quite grasp it. My eyes traveled the wallpaper-coated walls and high ceilings. Despite the fancy furnishings and crown molding, there were dark water spots everywhere. *And cobwebs in the corners*, I noted, shuddering again. *Please don't let there be many spiders here.*

Moments later, a scruffy man with white hair and a beard emerged, his wide neck and shoulders taking up the entire doorway between what appeared to be the kitchen and great room.

He nodded at me, frowning. "Nice to see you again, Norah. I pray you're staying out of trouble now?" he barked.

Taken aback, I could only nod. I looked over at Sara, but her eyes were elsewhere, staring up the steep set of red-painted stairs.

"Girls! Are you ready to come down and visit our guest, Norah?" she shouted.

I stiffened. There was something strange about the way she called me a "guest" instead of "Mom"; although perhaps that was only because she was calling out to both girls.

And why did she plan a playdate for Gemma on the same day she knew I was coming? I wondered, incredulously. I loved

15

the idea of Gemma making friends, but this was a big day for both of us. We hadn't laid eyes on each other in months.

Also, the word "visit" perturbed me. Yes, I had come as a temporary guest… but the plan was to take Gemma with me when I left.

I'm here for more than a "visit".

We still had a home in Chicago and a life to return to, and Gemma needed to be back there with her friends. Her real friends. And with me…

"Girls, answer your Aunt Sara now!" Francis boomed, giving me another jolt.

I stood up from the lounge, smoothing my plain black dress—the only dress I owned—and cleared my throat. "It's okay, really. Why don't I just go up and see her? That way she can keep playing with her new friend," I suggested. My foot was already on the first stair when Francis said, "Wait, Norah. Let's leave them to play. Why don't we take this opportunity to chat one-on-one instead?"

"Oh." I felt a flash of irritation, at having to wait even longer to see my daughter. *But I'm here now; a few more minutes of waiting won't kill me. I need to be patient and try to get along with my aunt and uncle.* Reluctantly, I followed them into an enormous kitchen and through an arched doorway that opened into a dark-paneled dining room.

Francis was already taking a seat at the head of the table. Nervously, I pulled out one of the heavy, highbacked chairs and took a seat several places away from him. The tabletop was covered in dusty bone china and bonafide napkins— the real kind, made of cloth.

There was a jaw-dropping chandelier in the center of the ceiling above the table, but like everything else, it was wobbly and stained. The whole place had an air of decay to it. A memory came floating back to me—a Dickens novel I'd read once, about a sad lady with a crusty old wedding cake rotting in the center of her dining table...

Something about this place set my teeth on edge.

Francis waited for Sara to sit down before he spoke. Once again, I tried to catch my aunt's eye from across the table, but she remained eerily quiet and standoffish in the presence of her husband.

"Now that you're here, I think it's time we lay down the rules," my uncle said, gruffly.

Chapter Three

STEP 2: FAITH

My uncle had made the rules very clear.

Some of those rules were expected: no alcohol or drugs.

Others were a little odd, but not unreasonable: no visitors, no social outings, no phone calls to friends in Chicago.

Granted, some of his rules were overreaching. I wasn't a child; rather, a grown woman, who had experienced more life lessons than most women twice my age.

It was the last rule that really bothered me: no alone time with Gemma.

At least not until we've developed some trust, my uncle had said.

In that moment, I had wanted to charge up those stairs, toss my daughter over my shoulder and run all the way home to Chicago. Who were these people to tell me what to do? To insist on controlling my current relationship with my own daughter—the daughter I grew in my womb and raised for the first six years of her life?

But I'd taken a deep breath and imagined myself floating on my back down the river... the way one of my counselors at rehab taught me. If I had to play by their rules for a little while, so be it.

I wasn't innocent in all this; I'd lost custody for a good reason. *But now I'm sober and taking my mental health meds as prescribed... what more do they want?*

———

It wasn't until dinner time that I saw my daughter. Feigning patience, I'd offered to help Aunt Sara in the kitchen. While she boiled potatoes and stirred stew, I peeled cucumbers for the salad.

I froze, paring knife mid-air as the tinkling sounds of children's laughter and small feet rocketing down the stairs filled the house. *Finally.*

I set the knife down, rubbed my hands on my sides, and followed the happy sounds. But as soon as I turned the corner, I came face to face with Uncle Francis. He blocked my path and turned to the girls. After his "rules" proclamation earlier, he was the last person I wanted standing between me and my daughter.

Francis boomed, "What did I say about running, ladies?"

"Sorry, Uncle Francis," the girls sang in unison.

I stepped around the hulking man to look at my

daughter. Smiling, I tried to hide my surprise at the changes in her appearance. Gemma was wearing a collared white dress, stiff with starch. Vastly different from the superhero tank tops and stretchy shorts she wore at home. And her hair… It was shorter. Much shorter. *Those bastards cut my baby's hair.*

Gemma's face broke into a silly grin and as soon as she came toward me, I was on my knees, reaching for my little girl. "Oh, angel. I missed you so much." I held her head to my chest, stroking her newly cut brown locks. How many times had I dreamed of this moment in rehab? To smell her milky-girl skin, touch the too-soft ringlets of hair…

Gemma had always been so fond of her long curls, that it seemed strange that she would want to cut it short above her chin. But maybe she had changed her mind… *After all I've been gone from her life for three months. What do I know, really?*

I leaned back so I could see her better, cupping her sweet cheeks in my hands. Running my fingers through her sweet, brown curls. The haircut suited her face, with its delicate elfin features and wide green eyes that matched mine and my mother's. *They match Sara's too*, I realized.

"I missed you too, Mommy." As Gemma spoke, I noticed that she had lost both her front teeth. *Oh, how much I have missed over these last few months*, I thought, sadly.

I didn't care what anyone said. Being an addict didn't necessarily make you a bad parent. I still loved my daughter and cared for her every day, until… until the drugs took over completely.

I was a good mother once. *I'll be an even better mother this time…*

"How have you been?" My voice shook with grief and emotion.

Gemma shrugged. Another brunette stepped up beside her, looking back and forth between us, curiously.

"And you must be Susie," I smiled. Susie was pale, her skin translucent, blue veins peeping through her eyelids and cheeks. The young girl nodded, shyly.

"No more drugs?" Gemma asked, catching me off guard.

My face fell and immediately I looked over at Francis to confirm my worst fears. *Did they really tell my seven-year-old daughter about my drug use? How dare they?*

Francis merely shrugged.

"No more, I promise," I whispered, eyes wet as I pulled Gemma in for another hug.

"Come along now, my silly goose. You don't want to miss supper." Sara, who I hadn't even noticed had joined us, placed a firm hand on Gemma's shoulder. I watched as she steered my daughter away to the dining room.

Susie gave me a small, timid smile then ran after them.

"You told her?" I whisper-shouted, turning to Francis, who was still standing watchfully by the chaise lounge. "I thought we agreed that she was too young. I told her I was feeling ill, that I had to go away for a little while until I felt better…"

He crossed his arms over his chest. "We didn't actually agree on anything, Norah. And I'm fairly sure she already knew. That sort of behavior isn't something you can keep hidden. Surely you know that by now…"

My uncle walked off, leaving me standing there with my mouth hanging open.

_____

Scooping stew and bread into my mouth, I could barely taste it. My eyes lingered on Gemma, who was seated at the other end of the table beside Susie. They were whispering conspiratorially, clinking their spoons together, and there was a warm, satisfied feeling in my chest as I watched her playing like a happy little girl, as she should be.

Sure, my aunt and uncle might be a little strange and old-fashioned—and they cut my daughter's hair and told her more about my recovery than they probably should have—but at least they had provided her with a safe home while I worked on getting better.

I tried to force myself to relax, to feel gratitude, as I finished off my supper in silence.

But as much as I tried to convince myself that I should feel grateful, I couldn't shake the feeling of unease. The house was rundown, and my uncle was strict. But could it be that he was just old-fashioned? And the house was quaint and rural, albeit crumbly and isolated…

No matter how desperately I wanted to feel good about this place and these people, I couldn't deny my unease.

All I wanted to do was take Gemma aside and talk to her one-on-one. She'd written that letter about hating it here, and I wanted to know why exactly. I wanted to talk to her. To run outside and play, to hold her in my arms and cuddle her like we used to in our apartment on nights before our whole life was ripped apart... to apologize for being gone all these months...

Trust. My uncle's words from earlier floated back to me as I gathered up my dinner dish and reached for my aunt and uncle's plates too. *He said that I need to earn their trust, which isn't wholly unreasonable...*

"Oh, dear. You don't have to do that," Sara said.

"I know, but I want to. You made a lovely meal. The least I can do is wash up." After I'd cleared their plates, I cleared Gemma and Susie's too. I was disappointed when Gemma jumped right up and took off back up the stairs with Susie.

At least she's adjusting well, I thought, as I gently piled the dishes in the sink.

Finn was not her father, but she'd known him and grown close to him over the last two years... A terrible idea, on my part—bringing someone new into our lives.

And she knew he was gone forever.

Initially, I'd thought bringing Finn into our lives was a good thing for both of us. Oh, how wrong I was.

I became pregnant with Gemma at seventeen; the father was a boy I went to high school with. He was never involved, opting to leave for college less than a month before Gemma was born. So, her biological father was a deadbeat and the one man she'd seen me with was dead. The last thing I wanted to do was create any more trauma in

24

Gemma's life. Taking her back home to Chicago needed to be a smooth transition, as easy on her as possible. My aunt and uncle were right about that, even if they weren't what I was expecting.

Gemma deserves a mother who is healthy and sober. She deserves a happy home with me and her, no one else this time.

Determinedly, I scrubbed the heavy soup pot with a mesh sponge. My aunt and uncle's rules were ridiculous, but surely, they wouldn't last long?

I'd do whatever it took to win them over. How hard could it be to gain their trust?

Chapter Four

When the dishes were done and the food was all cleared, I seized the opportunity to excuse myself.

"If it's okay with you, I think I'll retire to my room. Unpack, maybe take a shower…"

Aunt Sara stood with her back pressed to the counter, a dainty cup of tea in both hands. Uncle Francis had disappeared after the plates were cleared; he seemed like the kind of man who considered cooking and cleaning up "women's work".

"That sounds fine, dear. Your suitcase is still in the library," Sara said. By library, I presumed she meant the dusty sitting room at the front of the house with all the books and creepy decorations.

I'm not sure why I expected her to escort me to my room; there was something so antiquated about this visit, this house, that I'd come to expect it.

"Your room is upstairs. Second door on the left." Sara's

eyes were glossy and distracted, and the way she held onto that teacup, as though it were the only thing keeping her still, reminded me of my own mother, jittery and nervous-like in the kitchen of our childhood home.

They'd been close once, Sara and my mother, Beth, before my mother's diagnosis. Over the years, I'd practically forgotten they existed. Until they showed up to rescue Gemma.

Part of me wanted to ask her then, about her and my mother's childhood. I never expected to lose my mom so young. *There are so many things I wish I had learned about her, so many questions to ask before she went...*

But I didn't ask Sara or bring up my mother. A part of me felt tired and strange, like an animal in a new habitat. Ninety days doesn't seem very long, but I'd grown accustomed to my life at the center—the routines, the meetings, the food, the isolation... *wash, rinse, repeat.*

Also, I didn't want to grow too attached here; to become too ensconced in this family. *I'll be leaving soon,* I reminded myself. *Maybe it's better if I don't ask too many questions while I'm here...*

"Thanks again for letting me come, and for watching over Gemma while I was away," I said, softly. Sara nodded, but she was still far away and dreamy, and I wasn't certain she had heard me.

In the library, I scooped up my luggage and made my way toward the steep, red staircase. The girls were still playing. I could hear the shuffle and whir of toys on hardwood, and laughter like Christmas bells floating from the rooms above.

Grateful for another moment with my daughter, I started climbing. But before I made it halfway to the top of the staircase, Francis bellowed from somewhere in the belly of the house, "Girls! Time to come downstairs. Susie, your mom will be here any minute! And Gemma, you need to finish your homework. Get ready for school tomorrow…"

School. I knew they had signed her up for first grade at the local public school, and I prayed she wouldn't miss her newly made friends when I transferred her back to school in Chicago. *We have so much to talk about, details to work out … and oh, how much I have missed. My daughter's first day of first grade, a moment I'll never get back…*

I sighed, reaching the landing just as the girls came bounding down a narrow hallway, straight toward me.

Susie flew on by me, tiny feet pounding the steps in a hurry to greet her mom. Gemma was set to follow, but she stopped beside me on the landing. She had grown taller, I noticed, her cheek at my hip-level now, and she grabbed onto my leg and squeezed so hard, like she never wanted to let me go.

"Oh, sweetheart." Again, I dropped down on my knees to see her, pulling her in for a tight squeeze. "I'm so happy to be here with you and I'm sorry I was gone for so long."

"Me too, Mommy." Her eyes darted toward the staircase. I could hear Francis somewhere down below, asking Susie where Gemma was. *Why does he seem so controlling? Am I being paranoid or is he really this ridiculous?!* I wondered.

"I got the letter you sent," I told Gemma. "Why do you hate it here?"

Gemma's eyes widened for a moment, and again, she glanced down the stairs, waiting for Francis to appear.

"I don't. I was just missing you when I wrote it, is all," Gemma said, breathily.

"I know, sweetie, and I'm sorry you had to stay here for so long. I'm hoping we can go back home soon...."

"Norah." This time when Francis spoke, his authoritarian tone was directed at me. He stood at the bottom of the stairs, hands resting on his broad hips.

"Go on, Gemma." I nudged the small of her back and watched her tiny legs as she pumped down the stairs toward Francis. He opened his arms, scooping her up when she reached the bottom. As Gemma giggled, his eyes lingered over her shoulder, pinpointing mine.

There was something cruel and territorial about those eyes... I turned away from him, clutching my suitcase in one hand, flexing my fingers into a fist with the other.

There was something about the way Francis interacted with Gemma that put me on edge. And, although I'd only been here for a couple hours, I was already wary.

To complain, or even to think bad thoughts about my aunt and uncle, felt like ingratitude at its finest. If it weren't for them, Gemma probably would have become a ward of the state, I reminded myself. *I'm grateful I'm grateful I'm grateful...*

But I simply couldn't shake the feeling. *Something about Francis... isn't right. Grateful or not, he's only her temporary guardian and he's acting like he's king of the castle.*

Like the ornate furniture with its semi-hidden layer of dust, and the damp chill that permeated the air, there was something rotten about my uncle, and perhaps the entire place.

Chapter Five

STEP 3: SURRENDER

A warm wave of relief washed over me as I closed the sturdy bedroom door behind me. The second floor of the house was smaller than I'd expected, housing two bedrooms, one bathroom, and a roomy playroom littered with toys. The second room on the left was across from the playroom, and next to the bathroom. A perfect location, if only Gemma were nearer.

I'd scouted out the other bedroom in passing. It was bare; obviously, Gemma was staying in a room downstairs closer to Francis and Sara. *Of course, they're not going to let me get too close to her; they probably don't trust me not to run off with her, or to relapse and do something stupid.*

That's the thing about being an addict. They tell you in AA that it's like a disease, something that can't be helped. Something that never fully goes away. But what they don't tell you is that the stigma is another piece you'll never be rid of—friends and family won't trust you, and every peak or valley in mood or behavior might be interpreted as "Oh no, she's using again."

Because, you see, diseases are easy to pinpoint. They show up on CAT scans and bloodwork... they can, sometimes, be treated and cured with medicine or surgery.

So, call it a disease all you want, but most people don't view it that way. Not really.

I'd certainly seen plenty of that in rehab—the stigma. It came from the staff and other residents' families who came to visit... sometimes, even other patients.

Wear it like a badge of honor, one of the ladies in my Tuesday group told me when I mentioned my concerns about stigma to the others. She'd bared her teeth at me, and I'd been forced to look away.

It doesn't feel like a badge to me. It feels like my past is carved into my skin, on the surface for everyone to see who knows me and in the deep for me to remember.

My aunt and uncle certainly don't trust me.

Hell, maybe there was a part of me that didn't trust me either.

Tossing my chintzy suitcase on the bed, I surveyed the room that would be mine for the unforeseeable future.

The room was spacious, half as big our entire apartment in Chicago. High ceilings, two fans. Crown molding. And like the rest of the house, lots of dust and water stains.

One side of the room sported rows of shelves. Half were filled with more of those creepy little knick-knacks, the other half with paperback books. Running my finger along the spines, I recognized a few of the titles—mostly mysteries I'd read as a child—but many I did not know. *Well, at least I won't get bored. There will be plenty of new books to choose from here, unlike the rehab center.* There had been a library of thirty-one worn-out books at the center, and there's only so many times you can reread Melville or Poe before your head feels thick with debris and the words run together...

A small door across from the shelves led to a deep walk-in closet. I tugged on a chain from overhead, and discovered that the bulb was out. *Doesn't matter. I don't have enough clothes to fill the dresser, let alone all these empty wire hangers.*

I shut the closet tight, an old habit from my childhood, and went to the bed. It was a four-poster, adorned with two wooden nightstands and covered in a needlepoint quilt that I couldn't help wondering if Sara had sewn herself.

My suitcase had been set in the center of the bed. Sighing deeply, I unhooked the latches and stared inside at my few meager belongings.

Right away, I could sense that someone had gone through my stuff. *But who, and when?*

The T-shirts and jeans that I'd rolled so tightly to make them fit were now blobbed together.

It was possible that things were shifted around during the car haul here, but it seemed unlikely...

I dug beneath my clothes, searching.

I'd placed my copy of the *AA Big Book* on top before I'd left the center, but now it was tucked underneath the cheap garments, one corner of the front cover bent.

Scooping the clothes all the way out, I rummaged through my underwear and toiletries, relieved when I found my skinny black electronic cigarette.

Undoubtedly, my aunt and uncle would never approve —but nicotine was the one thing I'd been unable to give up in rehab. Plus, everyone there smoked, making it more difficult to quit.

I took a long hit off the e-cig, a rush of relief shuddering through me as I peered down at my tousled belongings. *Did my aunt or uncle snoop through my bag?*

It seemed so wrong, but then again… I thought back to their rules and general mistrust. That boundless *stigma*. It wouldn't be that much of a stretch to think he, or she, checked through my things to make sure I wasn't bringing in alcohol or drugs.

I started to fold the clothes, place them in the dresser drawers—but then thought better of it. *I don't want to get too comfortable since I'm leaving soon.*

I re-rolled my shirts and pants, then carried the entire case down the hall to the washroom. The all-white bathroom with its cold square tiles seemed cleaner than the rest of the house, probably because it was rarely used.

The best part was the clawfoot tub. I'd planned on a shower, but this was better.

As I filled the tub with steaming hot water and shampoo for bubbles, I took the opportunity to check myself out in the mirror. Looking at myself was a rarity at the center; when you're sharing a bathroom with eight other women, there's very little room for privacy, much less vanity.

My cheeks were no longer hollowed out, and I'd gained nearly twenty pounds over the last ninety days. And although my long black hair was too long and out of style, the rest of me wasn't so bad.

It felt good, being back to the sober-me. But as soon as the thought was there, it dissipated. I missed Finn fiercely; those early days when we were happy and free before the drugs took over completely had felt so carefree and good…

I stared in the mirror at my body, naked, all but my silver chain around my neck. On it, my engagement ring from Finn. It was lightweight, but somehow it felt heavy. Always a reminder on my chest… a way to remember him.

———————————

It was the kind of meet-up you read about in magazines. Girl caught in the rain, boy saves the day with his umbrella. Finn was funny and kind, with a strange fuck-it-all style you couldn't pin down. And he was ridiculously likable.

That day, in the rain with Finn, I thought he was walking me home to my apartment building, only to discover he lived there too. We were only one floor apart all that time—and we met in a rainstorm two blocks away, almost like it was fate. Like we were supposed to meet all along.

The drugs came later. A small piece of Finn, a part he had "under control". I'd like to say I tried them out of peer pressure, or because there was something missing inside me, but the truth was, I'd never been in love before. The drinking, the drugs—those were all secondary to my real addiction: Finn himself. I was wrapped up in him and willing to do anything, try everything, during those happy early days. It felt like nothing was wrong, nothing could *go* wrong, when I felt that happy.

Partying with Finn came new to me; my early high-school rebellion days had been short-lived. My days and evenings were filled with work and Gemma, no time for being foolish. But then Finn came along; he made responsibility and careless fun both seem possible. And he replaced the hole in my chest left by the death of my mother. Like me, she'd been a single mother doing it all alone, and I thought, after having Gemma, that at least I'd have her around to help me. To be my one ally in this world...

Finn was that replacement, my other half.

Finn adored Gemma and she took a liking to him too. For a while, things were good. Really good. Until I realized the drugs weren't a simple party favor on Saturdays for Finn; they were a daily habit. And much to my own horror, I realized that my body needed them too; a frighteningly obvious fact that I should have predicted but never thought I had to worry about.

I'd always thought addiction was a choice. But my body, sweating and convulsing there at the end—my body let me know that *it* was in control, no longer me.

I opened my small pack of toiletries and forced myself to follow through on my nightly routines and not allow my thoughts to stray. Brush, floss, pluck. *Wash, rinse, repeat.*

Satisfied, I turned the water off and climbed in the heavy cast-iron tub. Moaning with delight, I lowered my body slowly, remembering how good it felt to bathe rather than shower, and how lovely it was to have this moment alone.

I leaned back in the tub, resting my neck against the back and closing my eyes. For a split second, I could almost imagine this were my own house; that it was only me and Gemma, and I was relaxing after a hard day of work…

Work was another thing I was worried about. I was working on my teaching certificate before my arrests and before I lost Finn.

Is teaching even an option anymore? I wondered. With my addiction and mental health issues, I wondered if any school would trust me to teach their kids. I'd been working at a local restaurant while studying, earning pretty good tips. It wasn't the worst job, but I'd hoped it was only temporary until I finished my certificate. Now I was back at square one, unsure what to do next in regard to my career goals.

Mom was so proud of me for going to school. She came from a blue-collar family, her dad working on the assembly line at the Ford Plant. She'd paid our bills with her tips from Tony Tomato's Family Diner. My mother hadn't attended college.

The only consolation to her death is that she didn't have to see how far I'd fallen. Her disappointment and heartache over my addiction would have killed her just as fast as the cancer, probably.

Feverishly, I scrubbed my arms and chest, trying to rid

myself of the thoughts. *One day at a time,* one of my mentors had told me. *Don't get stuck there in the past. You have to move forward now…*

But that was easier said than done.

The water that felt so soothing moments earlier, now felt too hot… It was like the tiny walls of the bathroom were closing in on me. I tugged on the drain and stepped out, drying off with a fluffy gray towel I'd found in a short stack under the sink.

I slipped on the only nightgown I owned and twisted my hair up into a towel.

As soon as I returned to my room, I climbed under the thick quilt and closed my eyes. It was barely nine thirty, but I was physically and emotionally drained after the day and an early night's sleep sounded like a good idea.

Hours later, my thoughts were drifting, heady and strange when I heard a thump from overhead. My eyelids flew open, my brain taking a second to catch up to my whereabouts.

Thump.

Slowly, I pushed the covers down and sat up in bed. The room was velvety black, the only light a thin sliver of moonlight sneaking in from the window… *I didn't turn out the lights before I lay down, I'm certain of it. If I didn't turn them out, then who did?*

Shivering from my still wet, tangly hair, I got up and went to the bedroom door. It was still locked from the inside, so no one could have messed with the lights…

Thump.

My eyes drifted up to the ceiling again.

I hadn't even realized there was a third floor. *An attic full of rats, perhaps?*

The hairs on the back of my neck stood on end, and like a small child, I ran, leaping back into bed and tugging the covers over my face.

Chapter Six

I n the light of the day, the dusty nooks and crannies, the peeling wallpaper... they almost looked cozy and quaint. For a moment, I could imagine I was on vacation—overnighting at some isolated inn, with a grandmotherly innkeeper and a hot-plated breakfast waiting for me.

Fingers fumbling through the covers, I tried to find my phone. I'd barely looked at it since arriving yesterday, and I was surprised to find that it was after nine in the morning.

I opened a text message from my service provider. Disconnection, due to non-payment. Wish I could say I was surprised. Last night I'd checked my bank balance when I couldn't fall back to sleep. The number was the same, no matter how hard I willed it to change: 20.72 in checking.

Tossing the phone aside, I sat up in bed. Too fast, my head spinning. *How did I sleep so late?*

But then I remembered the strangeness of last night—the mysterious thumps and the light turning itself off. *Did I turn it off or did someone come in my room?* The thought of my uncle poking his head in while I was sleeping gave me the creeps.

I'd slept heavily… or had I? Part of me felt like I hadn't slept at all.

In rehab, my day started at 6.30. Breakfast, shower, groups. Then chores and lunch, followed by individual therapy and more groups. I'd grown so accustomed to the annoying dinging of bells, the rustle and groans of my fellow housemates, the daily schedule, that I hadn't even thought about setting an alarm last night.

I closed my eyes, listening for sounds coming from downstairs. Showers and cooking, warbled voices through the vents—I could hear none of that. In fact, I could have heard a pin drop, the house a tomb.

Soundlessly, I tossed the covers back and slipped out of bed. Tiptoeing down the steps, I drifted through the foyer and library. Wandered through the empty kitchen…

"Anyone home?" I asked, quietly, not really expecting a response. It was obvious they had all left; probably Francis had gone to work, and Sara had taken Gemma to school.

I wished they would have awakened me, but I should have been smart enough—responsible enough—to set my own alarm. I would have loved to have seen Gemma off to school… to have seen where she spent her days…

"Hello?" I said again, my own voice low, unfamiliar.

One by one, I entered the first-floor rooms, each more soundless and vacuum-sealed than the next.

I peeked my head into a large master, which

undoubtedly belong to Francis and Sara. The bed was neatly made, the ornate dresser and hope chest spotless. I could imagine Sara waking up early, carefully making her bed. Sweeping away forgotten clothes... My own mother had been hell-bent on routine when I was growing up, picking up everything behind me, sometimes before I was even done using it. I wondered if Sara were much the same.

I didn't dare step inside their personal bedroom, in case one of them were home after all.

Moving past the master, I discovered two more rooms. Both were neat but didn't appear to be in use. *Where does Gemma sleep?* I wondered, not for the first time. It wasn't until I reached the end of the hall that I found my answer.

A narrow door revealed a twisted stairwell that led to another second floor. This floor was detached from mine, its own separate suite.

It was here that I found remnants of my daughter—her sweet, honey smells. Her clothes from last night tossed on the floor in a careless pile. The room was simple yet cozy; a brassy twin bed was pushed against a window with a pleasant view of the back garden. A velvet wing chair set in the corner. An armoire carved with daffodils and lilies stretched to the slanted ceiling above. And a beautiful white desk stacked with books—Harry Potter, Percy Jackson... even some old classics, *Huckleberry Finn* and *Tuck Everlasting*.

I paged through them, taking a whiff of the ink and paper as I did when I was Gemma's age. She had a bookmark in *Tuck Everlasting*, keeping her page. I closed my eyes, memories floating back of baby Gemma in her swing, rosebud lips puckered and her undeveloped eyes still black as coal. Even though she was only a month old, I liked to read to her. I didn't have much money then, so I'd trek down to the local library and borrow as many books as they would allow, then perch on the floor beside her swing, reading them one after the other...

Of all the stories I'd heard and read about on motherhood, no one prepared me for the fear. Fear she'd stop breathing. Fear she wouldn't be smart. Fear that I'd screw her up, seeing as I was a poor teenage mom who barely graduated before she was born.

Seeing these books here, strewn across the desk, filled me with a sense of pride. I always hoped she'd be a reader.

I knew Gemma was smart for her age, but these books seemed advanced—I felt impressed, the corners of my lips curling into a little smile. *She's going to be okay. I might have fucked up for a little while, but my little girl is smart and safe and kind—and that's all that really matters.*

Circling the room, I couldn't help making comparisons to Gemma's cramped bedroom in Chicago. Her bedroom was basically half of my room, separated by a divider. It consisted of a twin bed and one dresser.

I sat down on the beautiful, brassy bed, springs groaning beneath my weight, and I smoothed out my daughter's covers.

How lovely for Gemma to have this view, this bed and this desk... all those books... Oh, I would have loved this as a young girl. Imagining secret fairies and mystical happenings out there from my garden view, getting lost in stories—old and new.

Seeing Gemma's room provided me with a small sense of relief. Sure, my aunt and uncle were a little strange, but they had provided her with this lovely bedroom. *They haven't been mistreating her, at least.*

I tried to remember staying in this house as a child, but I kept drawing a blank. My only memories here were of me and mother in the garden, brief flashes of Aunt Sara's smile...

Remember—Gemma said she hates it here, I reminded myself.

But Gemma's room was beautiful. And whether she hated it or not, Sara and Francis had kept her clothed and fed, and provided her with a lovely room full of books...

Gemma had explained her letter yesterday—she only said it because she missed me at the time, which made perfect sense. *Surely that's all it was?* I hoped.

Pressing my face to the windowpane, I imagined how I looked up here to an outsider. Like a tiny doll peering out from her doll house window to the big world outside...

Aunt Sara. Through the glass, I could see her. Bent at the waist, she was tugging on something in the dirt behind the Belladonna statue.

I don't know what possessed me to do it, but I unlocked the tiny window and tried to slide it open. It was stuck, only budging halfway. Before I could call out to her in the garden, I heard voices, carrying in the wind all the way up to me...

Who is she talking to?

Moments later, Sara stood, briefly, stretching her back and legs, and I saw a cell phone tucked between her shoulder and cheek.

"Honestly…" and I could have sworn I heard Francis's sister's name: *Merrill.* "I don't know what to think. I'm not sure if she's actually sober. I mean, how much can we trust these people at the clinic? Maybe they just needed an open bed and were ready for her to move on…"

This version of Aunt Sara was different than the meek and mild, overly polite woman I'd met last night.

Stung by her cruel words, I tugged the window shut and turned away. My eyes burned with embarrassment, flooding with tears. *I can't listen to one more word of that.*

The thought of Sara relaying everything back to her sister-in-law, gossiping amount me, and making *incorrect* assumptions—it cut me to the bone. *So much for being able to trust Aunt Sara.*

Moments later, I was back downstairs, and then up the steep red staircase to my own room, in my own wing. *They obviously want to keep us at opposite ends of the house because they don't trust me at all,* I thought, playing back Sara's whispery words in the garden.

By the time I'd gathered what I was looking for, changed my clothes, brushed my teeth, and prepared a bowl of oatmeal, Sara was back inside.

"Oh, there you are dear," she said, no trace of her earlier conversation in her voice. She was wearing a thick black pair of gardening gloves. She slipped them off, slowly, and moved to the kitchen sink where she began washing the dirt and grime from her hands.

"I've been up for a while," I said, keeping my voice even. "But I missed seeing Gemma off to school this morning. What time does she normally leave?"

"Francis drives her at 6.30," Sara said, her back still turned to me.

She had seemed so kind and inviting yesterday. But after seeing the way she changed around Francis last night and overhearing that catty call in the garden, I saw her in a brand-new light. And not a particularly flattering one, either.

Sara and Francis were obstacles—gaining their trust was one final hoop to get through before re-starting my life with Gemma.

"Thanks for telling me. I'll make sure I'm up early tomorrow so I can learn Gemma's school routine," I said, evenly.

Sara turned around and flashed a tight smile. "What are those?" She pointed at the thin stack of yellow papers I'd placed on the kitchen island.

"These," I said, flipping the first sheet over, "are my discharge papers from Crown Anthony. We were so busy last night, with our introductions and supper, that I didn't get the chance to give these to you and Uncle Francis."

"I see." Sara joined me on the other side of the island, licked her pointer finger, then flipped to the second page of the discharge packet.

"I thought, since you all have temporary custody of

Gemma, that you might like to see my final reports upon leaving the clinic. We go back to court soon, and I wouldn't blame you if you had doubts and concerns about me... See there? All of my final drug screens are listed, on page four, and my list of medications on five. And my doctor and therapist and group leader's notes... all of the progress I made while I was there... They were confident when they discharged me."

"Hmm." Minutes passed as Sara glanced through the pages. I leaned on one foot, then the other, feeling restless. I felt as though I were under a microscope.

"Ninety days," Sara finally said.

"Yes. Ninety days. Some people stay for shorter amounts, some longer... I stayed until they all agreed I was ready."

"That's great," she murmured. But the way she said it didn't make it sound so great.

"Ninety days doesn't seem very long, Norah." Sara's eyes rose to meet mine.

"Well, I'm not completely home free. I'll have to continue taking my medications—I take an SSRI for depression and another pill for anxiety, morning and night. And, of course, I'll be doing follow-up outpatient treatment in Chicago, and attending weekly peer support meetings." I cleared my throat.

Sara picked up the papers, straightened them, and then smiled. "That's wonderful, Norah. I'm so glad you're better. Honestly, I am."

"Thank you," I said. Sara came around the island,

drawing me in for a deep hug. Her long hair was fine as silk on my cheek, and it had a smell to it—like warm herbs and spices.

As hurt as I was by her words in the garden, I could understand them. *I have to give her reasons to trust me.*

"Now," Sara said, and in a moment of strange intimacy, she tucked a stray hair behind my ear and tapped my nose. "What will you do about work?"

"Work." Without thinking, I untucked that wild piece of hair. "Well, I'm close to being done with my teaching certificate. But I'm not exactly sure if I'll be able to go back to that quite yet, now that I have a record. However, I'm not too concerned about income. I mean, I am, but..." I took a breath, forcing my thoughts to slow back down. *That's the thing about my mental illness—thoughts either move too fast or too slow, never quite right...*

"I'm concerned but confident. Before I went into rehab, I waitressed at Leo's and I made pretty good tips there too. My old boss will take me back; in fact, I called her before I left for rehab just to be sure."

Sara raised one eyebrow. "And this Leo's—this is a place in Chicago?"

"Yes! It's only a couple blocks from our old apartment. And I left on good terms with my landlord there, too... He agreed to keep my stuff in the basement storage for me. And I'm sure they'll both take me back, my landlord and my boss..."

What I failed to say here: my landlord was a recreational drug user, who understood my pleas when I told him I was leaving for rehab. He had been fairly understanding and supportive.

"But…" Sara gave me a hard look, radiating something —a feeling I couldn't quite put my finger on.

"But what?"

"Is that really what you want? To return to your old life, I mean. And what about Gemma? I'm not sure it's healthy for her to go back there, to that apartment where… where that boy died. To the same job for you, where you'd probably have access to a bar and alcohol…"

I crossed my arms over my chest and pinched my eyes closed. *Breathe in, breathe out. Wash, rinse, repeat…*

"I see where you're going with this, Aunt Sara, and I get what you're saying, really, I do. But Chicago is our home. It's the only place Gemma's ever lived…"

"Until now," Sara clarified.

"Correct. And, just so you know, she wasn't there when Finn died. Thank goodness for that. She was with the sitter while I was at work. When I found him, she wasn't with me…" I could still see the blood. *Smell it.* Finn's death like a crime scene.

His heart stopped while he was standing, shooting up, and his body had crumpled, his head snapping on the beveled edge of the kitchen table… For a moment, I could almost imagine how it must have sounded: the dull thunk of his temple, connecting with the sharp edge…

I cleared my throat. "Gemma knows he's gone, but she was well insulated from these things—she didn't see it…"

"She knows more than you think, Norah."

Memories from last night fluttered back to me. Gemma's pleading voice, that mollifying look on Francis's face.

"I understand that she's been told things and you're right, she probably understands more than I realized, but I'm not completely ashamed, Sara. I think it's something important to discuss with her when she's older. My mental illness, my addiction—knowing that will help evaluate her own risks in the future. I made a mistake. That doesn't make me a monster—I'm trying to correct it."

When Sara didn't respond, I continued, "I don't want to sweep her back to the same old life, but I do want to get back to normal. Her normal school, her old friends, and a regular routine for me. A routine that includes treatment and meetings. I want nothing more than to stay clean and sober. I want to be a good mom for Gemma. That's all I care about now."

"But there will be old friends... old habits there in Chicago," Sara said, chewing her lip.

"Well, like I said, it won't be easy. I'll have to go to meetings and avoid triggers. I'll continue working the steps... I'm determined to make this work, Sara. I appreciate you all's help, I certainly do. But Gemma is my daughter, and I would like to take her home soon. Chicago is my home, and it's hers too..."

Sara walked off, disappearing into the foyer. For a moment I thought she was angry, and wouldn't be returning, but then she came back holding her purse.

"Do you have your driver's license?" She unzipped an old leather purse, taking out a set of heavy car keys.

I nodded.

"Would you like to pick up Gemma from school today? I'll write down the address."

"Absolutely. I'd love that," I said, surprised.

Moments later, I had the keys in hand, a note with Sara's scribbled directions in my jean pocket. Truth was, I didn't drive much in Chicago. Most places, I could walk or catch a bus to. But my license was valid, and I had driven Finn's Durango, the big moosy thing, a few times when he was too high to drive.

"I hope you know that I love Gemma, and you. I want to make sure I'm doing everything to help you both. Please know that I'm on your side, Norah," Sara said, as I stood at the door preparing to leave.

I swallowed, holding back tears. "I know. Thank you. Seriously, I appreciate all you have done. It means so much to me and Gemma..."

Sara nodded and waved me out the door. I was thrilled to have the opportunity to pick up Gemma and I suddenly felt better about my standing with Aunt Sara.

Sara's Taurus was smaller than the Durango. I placed my wallet on the passenger seat, along with the directions to Restoration Elementary, and I adjusted the driver's seat.

I hadn't expected this—following Sara's conversation with her sister-in-law in the garden and the inquisition in the kitchen, it was hard to believe she was actually letting me pick up Gemma from school. And her final words, about loving not only Gemma but me too, truly touched me.

The thought of having an aunt who loved and cared for both me and my daughter… well, it filled me with something I hadn't felt in so long—a sense of belonging and pride. *Perhaps they're not so creepy after all. Maybe I can trust Aunt Sara… It would be so nice to have an ally. Someone to lean on…*

I turned the radio up, chuckling at Sara's choice of indie rock, and I backed the Taurus down the gravel drive.

Sara had given me precise directions—school let out at 2.35 and all car-riders were to follow the signs and line up beside the far-right entrance of the school.

I'm sure Gemma will be happy to see you waiting for her, Sara had said.

I sure hoped so. Last night, Uncle Francis had made it very clear—*his stupid rules.*

No alone time with Gemma.

But I suppose, taking her to and from school doesn't really count as alone time. Does it?

Either way, I was glad Sara was trusting me to do it.

As I pulled away from the sprawling old house and steered the car down the twisty gravel driveway, leaving Aunt Sara behind, I couldn't help feeling a sense of freedom. The house was lovely, in an eerie gothic way, but it was temporarily relieving to escape from it. The countryside was beautiful, in its simplicity and starkness, but I missed the city. The towering buildings and the bustling crowds… *I never felt alone in Chicago.*

And that whole house has a strange dampness to it, something wet and cold that settles in the bones. Makes me feel icky inside. I could suddenly breathe again—like there was more air to go around.

As I whizzed by the cornfields I'd passed on my way into town, I couldn't help feeling a rush of happiness. Perhaps it was the boost of serotonin from my meds or the thrill of being behind the wheel again, but I couldn't help smiling. Aunt Sara was tough. But she was looking out for my daughter's best interests, like a good aunt should. And she'd bent the rules, letting me pick up Gemma on my own, after only twenty-four hours… Maybe I could trust her after all. The important thing was that I demonstrated that she could trust me.

Please know that I'm on your side, Norah. Aunt Sara's words played through my head like a soothing soundtrack.

I wasn't so sure about Francis, but Sara I thought I could trust—at least, to some extent.

Wind blew through my hair, the lead singer of Death Cab for Cutie's melancholic voice urging me on, as I followed Sara's directions to the letter.

A right turn on one road named after a tree; a left turn on another (also named after a tree). The rolling hills transformed into a tiny town—a handful of mom-and-pop shops: a laundromat, drug store, and eatery—and then I reached the first traffic light. I turned left, easing the Taurus up a steady hill. At the top, surrounded by a tall, wired fence, was Restoration Elementary.

It was a long, one-story, brick building—it could have been any school in small-town America, they all looked the same to me. Signs for parent drop-off and pick-up were easy to find. I followed the arrows, finally parking at the curb. *I can't wait to see Gemma's smiling face when she comes through those doors...*

I checked my watch. I was ten minutes early. No other cars in sight.

I placed the car in park, unhooked my seatbelt, and reached for my phone on the passenger seat. It was nearly dead, and since it was disconnected, I couldn't call out or text, much less peruse the internet. Sighing, I longed for a book to read. *Maybe I'll check out some of the books in the 'library' tonight, find something Gemma and I can read together...*

I reached for a book of CDs on Sara's back floorboard. Chuckling, I unzipped the booklet and started flipping through her CD collection. It had been years since I'd seen one of these—most people used their phones or satellite radio these days. But I had to appreciate Sara's old school choices—Rolling Stones, Janis Joplin, The Cure.

A loud thump on my window gave me a jolt, sending the book of CDs scattering onto the passenger's side floorboard.

"Oh! Hi," I stammered, restarting the car so I could roll the automatic window down.

"Can I help you?" a woman asked, looking strangely suspicious of me. She was wearing her short blonde hair in a cute, stubby ponytail, and she had on a neat, checkered sweater and khaki pants. She looked like a teacher, certainly.

"Yes! Hi, I'm Norah. Gemma Campbell's mother. My

aunt or uncle usually pick her up, but I'm back in town and they sent me to get her today. I hope I'm in the right line…"

The woman smiled, kindly. "Well, you're in the right place, Norah. But you're way too early. School doesn't let out until 3.15, and we don't recommend lining up until 2.50 at the earliest," she explained.

"Oh." Cheeks reddening, I looked around the deserted lot. "Is it okay if I park and wait? I'll just pull back up at 2.50…"

The woman nodded, chewing her lip. "Well, that would be fine … but you're also supposed to have a number displayed."

"A number?"

"Yes. It's a lanyard given out at the beginning of the school year, with your child's assigned class number. That way, when students exit the building, we can double check that they are getting in the correct vehicle…"

"Oh," I said, again. "Well, that sounds like a good safety precaution. You can never be too careful these days…" My cheeks were so warm; I couldn't help feeling foolish, and also a little annoyed. *Why did Sara tell me 2.35? Perhaps she was confused, but she also forgot about the student number…*

"Listen. Go ahead and park and come inside. We'll check your name on the approved pick-up list and double check with Gemma's Uncle Francis," she said, pointing to a row of empty spaces near the front of the building.

"Okay, great. Thank you." As I pulled into a parking space, my hands shook nervously. *Why do I feel like a criminal? I'm just picking up my daughter from school!*

After a few deep breaths, I gathered up my wallet and keys and locked the Taurus behind me.

The curly-headed woman was waiting a few feet away. She had a walkie talkie on her hip, and someone was belting out instructions for dismissal.

"Follow me," she said, walking briskly toward the school.

"Thanks again. And I'm so sorry about the confusion," I said, jogging to catch up with her as she shoved her way through the double glass doors at the front entrance.

My tennis shoes squeaked as we entered a wide corridor. The same old familiar smells of my youth—bleach and wax, BO, and greasy food—came rushing back to me. We passed by the cafeteria, dreary and empty, paper boats for French fries or hotdogs littering the floor and filling oversized trashed cans.

"Wait here," the lady said, stopping in front of a glassed-in office that could only belong to the principal. "I'll ask Mrs. Fulkerson. What's your name again?"

"Norah Campbell," I said, smiling stiffly as I found a seat on a bench outside the office. Memories of sitting outside the principal's office, waiting to get chewed out by my own awful principal—Mary Marcum—*Doctor* Mary Marcum, to be clear—came rushing back to me.

I was a good student in elementary school, but like so many other girls, things changed in high school. I was more focused on friends and boys, and I got in trouble a few times for skipping.

When boys act out in school, people call them class

clowns or stupid jocks or typical boys... *Boys will be boys.* But when girls do it, well, that's a whole other story. That old nursery rhyme about sugar and spice came to mind. *We are supposed to be nice and quiet and polite, bottling up our emotions like toxic waste.*

Needless to say, I was never good at keeping the lid on. My emotions would seep out of that bottle, sometimes exploding—internally, if I were lucky, but most times they came out...

None of my teachers were surprised when I wound up pregnant my senior year.

"Ms. Campbell?" A stern brunette, with a compact body and an angular face, peered out of the office doorway.

"Yes?" I stood, trying out another smile.

"You don't have permission to pick up Norah," she said, briskly. "In fact, you'll need approval from her guardians. Once we have that in place, we can assign you a parking pass with Gemma's class number. Please discuss that with them and have them contact us if they're willing to do that. In the meantime, her Uncle Francis or Aunt Sara will need to pick her up from school..."

I can't believe this. Here are these people—essentially, strangers—who barely know my daughter—the child I gave birth to—and they're holding her hostage from me. Part of me wanted to yell and scream—*give me my fucking daughter!*

But I had to play it cool. *Head up. Shoulders back. Lid on your emotions, Norah,* I reminded myself. And another voice, one of my fellow rehab members: *it's your own fault for getting into this mess.*

60

In a sense, it was true. When I chose the drugs and got locked up after Finn's OD, I essentially lost my authority in Gemma's life. *I'll have to jump through more hoops than I realized to get her back*, I thought, drearily.

Taking a deep breath, I said, "I completely understand, and I respect your rules. But, you see, my Aunt Sara is the one who sent me here to pick her up today, so I do have their permission. If you could just call her…"

"Ma'am," the woman, who I could only assume had to be the principal, put up a hand to stop me. I took a step back, surprised by her iciness.

"I've already spoken to Francis. His number is the primary point of contact. And he said that you lost custody of your daughter and don't have permission to take her out of school at this time. I just got off the phone with him before I walked out here." She looked me up and down, eyes taking in my scruffy black sweater and my too-tight jeans with the holes… In that moment, I'd never felt like more of a loser. I imagined other mothers, with their glossy smiles and neat clothes, lining up outside to get their sons and daughters…

"I see. There must have been some sort of miscommunication. I'll discuss it with them tonight. Thanks." I turned away quickly, eyes burning with embarrassment and fury.

"Mom!" When I looked up, there was Gemma. My sweet little angel, in a lime-green jumper, running toward me.

She was in my arms before the principal could stop her.

"You came to pick me up!" she squealed, smiling so big I could see all her newly missing teeth.

The principal tsk-tsked behind me. I let Gemma go and brushed off my jeans, awkwardly.

"Listen, Gemma. I'm really sorry. I wanted to pick you up, but there was a bit of confusion. I didn't know about the parking numbers, and I didn't talk to Francis first. He'll be picking you up today, but I'll see you very soon at home. I can't wait to hear all about your day…"

"All right, Miss Gemma. Time to get back with your group. It's almost dismissal time," the principal said, stepping between us. I couldn't help wanting to punch her in that moment. But, then again, I reminded myself—*she's just looking out for my daughter. She doesn't know me. All she knows is what that asshole Francis told her.*

Gemma's face fell and my heart felt like it was cracking in a million places. *I have to stop disappointing her.*

"Okay, Mom. See you then."

I watched her as she ran, zig-zagging through the hallway toward a neat line of students. They all looked to be around her age, six or seven.

"I'm Norah, by the way." I whipped back around to face the principal, sticking out my hand. Face still set with disapproval, she reluctantly took my hand in hers. Her grip was worse than holding a limp noodle.

"A pleasure. Now follow up with Gemma's guardians and get the proper permissions before coming up to school again," she said. Her words like daggers, she practically nudged me down the hallway and back out the door I'd come in.

As I made my way back to the borrowed Taurus, clutching the keys so tightly my knuckles turned white, I couldn't hold it in anymore. The tears came tumbling down, hot and stinging, and I thrust the driver's side door open— too hard. It clipped the side mirror of the car beside it.

"Fuck." Swiping at my cheeks, I examined the mirror on the red Honda for damage. There was none to be seen. *Thank God.*

In the car, the tears kept coming. *How could I be so stupid?*

But then again… *Why did Sara tell me to come? And why did Francis deny my having permission to pick her up when the principal reached him by phone?!*

Flustered, I dug through the center console and opened up the glove box, searching for tissues. The last thing I wanted to do was embarrass Gemma at school, having a meltdown in the school parking lot where anyone could see. But that's exactly what I was doing.

There was a soft thump on my driver's window; I expected another suspicious teacher, or perhaps the angry driver of the Honda whose mirror I'd clipped. But the lady standing by the window was smiling.

Wiping my eyes and nose with the back of my hand, I rolled my window down.

"Hi there! You must be Norah." Her smile morphed into a look of concern.

"Yes, hello. That's me. I'm Gemma's mother," I sniffed.

"Are you okay?" she asked, softly, glancing around the

school parking lot. Other cars were coming in, circling the building. Parents with *permission* to pick up their sons and daughters.

"Yes, so sorry. I'm fine. Just a little miscommunication with picking up Gemma. My aunt said it was okay, but apparently she didn't communicate with my uncle, and I wasn't aware of the policy regarding number signs, or parking permits, whatever they're called..."

The woman was tall and fit, legs reaching my driver's window. She stooped down, resting an elbow on the windowsill.

"I'm so sorry that happened. I'm Jana, by the way. I'm the counselor here at Restoration. I just love Gemma," she said.

"Oh!" I rubbed at my wet cheeks. "That's so lovely to hear. And it's great to meet you, Jana."

"I saw what happened with Mrs. Fulkerson in the office. Do you have a minute to chat?"

Surprised, I started clearing off the passenger seat for her to get in. But when I saw the strange look on her face, my cheeks lit up again. "Oh... did you want to meet inside...? Because I don't think Mrs. Fulkerson would like that very much."

Jana shook her head. "Actually, I'm leaving for the day. There's a coffee shop around the corner. Just hang a right when you leave the parking lot and drive straight for about three miles. You can't miss it. A cute little shop called 'Beans'. We can chat there. If that works for you."

"Sure. That sounds lovely. I'll meet you there," I said.

I rolled my window up, watching as the graceful, gazelle-like counselor walked to her car. I was meeting a counselor off schoolgrounds to discuss ... *what, exactly? Gemma's well-being?* I wondered.

All I knew was that I was grateful to be treated like an adult, a *parent*. And I was eager to see what she had to say. If something was wrong with Gemma, I certainly wanted to know about it.

Chapter Seven

STEP 4: SOUL SEARCHING

"She talks about you all the time." Jana stirred two lumps of sugar into her coffee, taking her time, then she reached for a porcelain bell of creamer. The coffee shop consisted of only three wooden tables and a counter, but it was cozy and sweet, cutesy jars of beans on the shelves and old-timey photographs displayed on the walls. The woman who'd brought our coffee had the thickest southern accent I'd ever heard, and she introduced herself with her full name: Mary Beth Coffer. *You just can't make names like that up*, I thought, smiling.

"I think she really missed you while you were away." Jana was still talking.

I'd missed so much of Gemma's life, even in those few short months, and it was good to know she'd missed me too. I wanted nothing more than to start over, get back to where we used to be...

Early life with Gemma was hard; being a new mom is hard for most women, I think. But being as young and inexperienced as I was made it worse. I didn't know how to change diapers or mix formula. I knew next to nothing about babies. But one thing was certain—I loved her so much that it terrified me. From the moment I held her, looked into her eyes, and took a whiff of her flaky, dark curls, I was overwhelmed with emotion. I know everyone says it—being a mom changes you—but I never truly believed it. Not until it happened to me. Within seconds of meeting my daughter, I knew I'd lay down my life for hers, with zero hesitation. And the constant thought of losing her or messing up... well, it was scarier than any horror movie I'd ever seen. When Finn came along, I'd grown confident. Gemma was older, easier, I could handle a relationship, take a little time for myself. I never expected that the person who would hurt my daughter would be *me*.

"I missed her too. It was hard being away from her. I hope she hasn't been in any trouble at school," I said, a nervous shake in my voice.

"No, not at all," Jana said. "When your aunt and uncle enrolled her, they told me about the recent death of her stepfather and your decision to enter treatment. Since then, I've been meeting with Gemma twice a week, just to see how she's coping with the new school, and the stress that comes from losing a parent."

I took a long sip of coffee. It scorched my tongue, but I didn't care. I hated that my aunt and uncle had given out so much personal information, and I considered telling her that Finn and I weren't technically married when it happened—but, also, there was a huge part of me that felt relieved. Relieved that someone from school was looking out for Gemma's mental health and well-being when I couldn't...

"Yes, that's true. My aunt and uncle took temporary custody while I was in rehab. But I'm clean and sober now. I have ninety days under my belt."

"Congratulations," Jana said. Her smile was soft, genuine. Instantly, I took a liking to her. "And I'm sorry for your loss. I can't imagine what it's been like for you."

"Thank you," I said, reaching for my cup again. My cheeks were still sore from my earlier sobbing session at school. *Don't cry don't cry don't cry...*

"I've been sober for nine years, myself. Alcohol and benzos, a lethal combination," Jana said, not bothering to lower her voice even though Mary Beth was nearby.

I set my cup down, examining her more closely. She couldn't be much older than me, perhaps thirty or thirty-five...

"Congrats to you too, then," I said. "And I appreciate you sharing that with me."

Jana nodded, then leaned over her cup. She blew steam off the top but didn't take a drink.

"I wanted to meet with you for a couple reasons, Norah. One, I wanted to assure you that Gemma is doing fine academically. She's an excellent student, above average in reading and proficient in all other subjects, according to her teacher."

I beamed. "I can't tell you how wonderful that is to hear."

"She is, however, withdrawn. Which isn't all that unusual. She's new and kids have different personalities... plus, it's been a tough year for her, with everything that has happened with her home life."

I winced. "I know."

"But I think she'll adapt and be fine, especially now that her mama is back."

There was a lump in my throat. It felt... *good*, hearing someone confident in my role. The *importance* of my role in Gemma's life. The judge, the principal... my own relatives. No one seemed to think I mattered anymore. One simple mistake and suddenly, I was a monster. And here I was, drinking coffee with a total stranger, feeling the boost of confidence that I'd been needing for weeks.

"Thank you. I hope you're right. I'll do everything I can to help, and hopefully, hopefully I can get this misunderstanding with Francis cleared up soon so that I can help out more with pick-ups and drop-offs."

"Well, I wanted to talk about that, too."

"The confusion at pick-up?" I ripped open a packet of Sweet'n Low, bracing myself for another scolding.

"Francis."

My spidey senses tingled. *What if I'm not the only one who senses something off about that man?*

"What about him? Did something happen?"

Jana frowned. "No, nothing happened. But I've tried to engage with him and Sara multiple times, to discuss Gemma's behavior, her seeming a little sad and withdrawn... and I tried to suggest additional services."

"Like therapy?" I asked. With my own mental health and addiction issues, I, for one, was thankful for counselors and addiction specialists, and people like Jana who worked with school-age children. Getting extra services sounded like a *good* idea for Gemma.

"Yes. I wanted to give them a few referrals for local psychologists and discuss the importance of allowing Gemma to talk about Finn and to talk about you."

"Me?"

"Yes. She confided in me during one of our weekly meetings that she didn't feel comfortable talking about you with Sara and Francis. She feels like every time she brings you up, they become angry," Jana said.

I groaned. "For some reason, that doesn't surprise me... What did they say about the referrals you gave them?" I could feel my blood pressure rising, irritation with Gemma's temporary guardians (*they were supposed to be looking out for her, doing what's best for her, dammit!*).

"That's just it. I called Sara first, during the middle of the school day. She seemed friendly and open to the idea. But when Francis came to pick up Gemma the following day, he all but tossed the list back in my face and told me to back off."

I sat back in my chair, stunned. "I'm sorry he did that.

And I'm grateful you care enough about Gemma to want to help."

Jana nodded, solemnly. "I do. I care about her very much. She's a sweet girl. And, just so you're aware, she gave me permission to speak with you. I would never break her trust."

"She did?" It wasn't all that surprising, but it felt good to know Gemma still trusted me.

"She did. But Francis, on the other hand... Well, he specifically advised us, before you came back to town, *not* to speak with you. He also made sure we knew that you didn't have permission to pick up Gemma from school at any time. Which is why I was surprised when I saw you in the hall with Mrs. Fulkerson and realized who you were."

I could feel my jaw tensing, teeth grinding into dust. *That asshole.*

"Look, I know they have custody. But it's only temporary. And it's not like I'm some sort of monster! I had issues, and then I lost the man I loved. I went to treatment, I got better, I'm clean now..."

"I know, I know..." Jana reached across the table, surprising me, as she covered my hand with her own. She had lovely nails, like little half-moons painted petal-pink.

"Trust me, I know how you feel. It took me a long time to regain the trust of my family and friends... the community... and that's another reason I'm reaching out. There's an AA meeting every Saturday at noon at the church on the corner of Barberry and Maple."

"More berry and tree names, I see..." I smiled. "I'd love

to come. It never occurred to me to look for meetings around here."

"It's a small town. But we have our fair share of suffering and addiction, too. Around here, it's just not as acceptable to talk about... and harder to find meetings and support for," Jana admitted.

I'd never considered that. Growing up in a populated city, there were AA meetings everywhere—church basements and community centers...

"And if you need a sponsor, or just a friend in a time of a need... well, I can be there or make other suggestions. Here's my number." Jana reached into her purse and took out a business card with her cell phone number on it. She slid it across the table to me.

"Thank you," I said. And I meant it. The last thing I expected to find in this town was an ally, most certainly not another fellowship member. "I'll be there Saturday. Also, I can talk to Francis tonight if you'd like, about those referrals..."

Jana's face settled into a grim line. "Let's hold off on that part for now. I don't want to make things worse for you or Gemma. For today, I'm just glad we connected. And I'm hoping we can discuss more about Gemma in the future."

"See, the thing is..." After all her kindness, I hated to tell her the truth. "We're not planning on staying long. My ultimate goal is to take Gemma home to Chicago, the sooner the better."

If Jana was surprised, she didn't show it. In fact, she had

a faraway look in her eye—as though there was something else on her mind, something else she wanted to tell me...

"I think taking Gemma back is a good idea, although I have a feeling Francis won't make that easy," she said, surprising me with her candor.

I nodded, finishing off my coffee. She was right. But as long as I was clean and I didn't do anything between now and our court date next week, then I couldn't see a judge refusing a reunion between Gemma and me. Courts were supposed to be in favor of reuniting families, and usually mothers had the advantage from my experience.

"Francis seems almost possessive of Gemma, and not in the way a temporary guardian should be, to be frank," Jana added.

Again, my insides were churning, those tingly glitches of fear rising up from under my skin.

"That was my initial impression, too. We go back to court soon though..."

"Well, if you need a lawyer let me know. I know a couple who live in the area," Jana offered, keeping her face impassive as she sipped her coffee.

The last thing I could afford was a good lawyer, or *any* lawyer, in fact. My thoughts returned to my waning bank balance and it suddenly occurred to me that I couldn't even call her from my cell if I wanted to, seeing as it had been disconnected.

"Thank you. I may take you up on that," I said, softly. Moments later, we were saying our goodbyes. Jana hugged me—I'd been hugged more times in the last twenty-four hours than I had in several months—and reminded me one last time about local AA meetings.

"I'll be there," I said, climbing back behind the wheel of the Taurus. I tucked her card inside my coat pocket, feeling a mixture of pleasure at meeting a new friend and fear that my initial concerns about Francis were correct.

Chapter Eight

STEP 5: INTEGRITY

U ncle Francis blocked the doorway with his body as I mounted the steps on the porch.

I'd expected some weird excuse about not letting me pick up Gemma, but I hadn't expected this.

"The rules were clear. No alone time with Gemma. Not until you've earned our trust," Francis barked.

"How exactly am I supposed to do that, if you won't let me take over some of the responsibilities related to her, huh?"

Francis flinched, as though I'd slapped him. "You've been here less than twenty-four hours and already you're causing trouble."

My fingers curled into fists. He was blocking the entrance; inside, I could hear the clanking of plates, the soft murmurs of Sara and Gemma eating dinner.

Lowering my voice to a whisper, I tried to explain: "Aunt Sara handed over the car keys and told me to go get her. She even wrote out directions. What was I supposed to do? Call and ask your permission after I already had it from her?"

Francis shook his head in disgust, whether with me or Aunt Sara, I couldn't be sure. Probably both.

What the hell is his deal? Furthermore... why didn't Aunt Sara explain this to him? Why didn't she defend me? Is she so far under his thumb that she's afraid to tell him she gave the okay for me to do the pick-up?

Remembering the concerns Jana had voiced over coffee earlier, I wanted to pummel this man. Was he getting off on this? Some sort of power trip over my family?

Every inch of me wanted to fight back, argue... but I forced myself to take deep breaths. *I'm grateful I'm grateful I'm grateful*, I chided. But, in reality, I didn't feel grateful at all. These people were supposed to be on my side. They were supposed to be *family*.

I swallowed my anger. "Look, I'm sorry for the confusion, Uncle Francis. I really am. I thought I was being helpful by picking her up."

Francis raised one eyebrow, thick and pokey like a caterpillar. He moved aside, but only enough that I still had to rub against his shoulder to get by. The man smelled musty like the rest of the house; like a damp blanket left in the dryer too long.

"Where else did you go? We've been home for nearly an hour; we've already sat down for supper."

My eyes narrowed as I scooted past him. "I had no idea you all ate so early." I tried to force my voice to stop shaking. Francis was a large man, nearly a foot taller than me, and certainly much wider. But despite his girth, I wouldn't let him intimidate me. *I've been through worse hell than this man could ever dish out.*

"I'll make sure I'm here for dinner tomorrow. I want to spend as much time with Gemma as possible. And I went for coffee. Truthfully, I was a little shaken up after what happened at the school. The principal was very rude to me."

"Coffee. By yourself?"

I nodded, my stomach twisting with unease. *I'm not the child here. Why is he treating me like I am?*

But if there was one good thing I'd learned from being a junkie, I knew how to lie when I needed to.

"Yes. I saw the cutest little coffee shop after I left school, a place called 'Beans'. The coffee was good, but the best part is that I found a flyer on their bulletin board. I'm going to attend AA meetings at the church near Barberry Street."

Uncle Francis looked me up and down, assessing my reliability. "What church is it? There's a few down there," he said, rubbing his chin.

"Umm..." I tried to remember the name of the other street Jana mentioned. "I'm not exactly sure."

"Well, do you have the flyer on you? Probably says on it."

And that's the bad thing about being a junkie and a liar; after a while, you get caught trying to maintain your own deceptions.

"I didn't save the flyer. I left it hanging on the board. I

guess I'll have to ride down there on Saturday and stop in the churches on Barberry Street at noon, 'til I find the right one." *How many churches could there be?* I wondered.

Francis smiled at me, showing all his teeth. "I'd be happy to drive you on Saturday."

"Thank you," I responded, tightly.

"Now let's eat." I let Francis lead the way. Following him into the dining room, I smiled tightly at Gemma as I shed my coat and draped it over the back of the chair. Sara sat opposite Gemma, and when I glanced her way, she refused to meet my eye.

"How was school today, sweetie?" I asked.

Gemma's plate was full of mashed potatoes doused in gravy. I scooped some potatoes onto my own plate and waited for Francis to pass the plate of meatloaf my way.

"Good," Gemma said. Her eyes were downcast, focused on the mountain of gravy she wasn't eating. She picked at the hill with her fork, her other hand in a small fist pressed to her cheek.

"It looks like a nice school," I said, reaching across the table to touch her elbow.

"Don't play with your food," Francis warned her.

Gemma, without looking at me, sat up straighter in her chair and filled her mouth with a huge bite of potatoes on command.

My thoughts circled back to my conversation with Jana. She had described Gemma as 'withdrawn'. I tried to picture my little girl through someone else's eyes. Right now, she seemed sullen, quiet. *What if she has no friends at her new school?*

Just the thought of it gave me a sharp pain in my chest. *Poor Gemma. This is all my fault. She was suddenly whisked away to a new state, a new school—a brand-new family. All because of my bad choices.*

"Do you have friends at Restoration? I met your principal and a couple teachers. They seem nice," I lied, thinking back to that snooty Mrs. Fulkerson. That woman took one look at me and passed judgment. But really, could I wholly blame her for it?

Gemma finished chewing, then said, "I have some, I guess. I miss my friends back home, though."

I smiled, sadly. "I know you do, baby. Hopefully, you will get to be back with them soon."

Sara cleared her throat loudly but said nothing. It was Francis who spoke up for her. "Let's not make any promises until things have been decided. Okay?" he said, giving me a warning look.

That's the thing about men like Francis. They take up the whole room with their presence and power, trying to make everyone around them feel small. But I couldn't help feeling most hurt by Sara—*why did she set me up to fail today? Did she do it on purpose?*

I could tell Gemma felt uncomfortable; I could sense the tension in her shoulders and back, stiffening as Francis laid eyes on her again. Suddenly, it couldn't have been any clearer to me—*we have to get away from this man. If Sara wants to put up with his controlling, pompous ass that's her problem. My daughter and I shouldn't have to.*

"Francis is right," I said, through clenched teeth. "We have to go back to court first and get things cleared away. In the meantime, we are lucky to have a place to stay and a decent school to go to. But I do know this has been hard on you, honey. And I'm so sorry for that. I'll get you back to your friends as soon as I can."

I sensed Francis wasn't happy with this statement either, but I didn't care.

Gemma glanced up at me, then back at her plate.

"How about homework? Is there anything I can help with tonight?" I asked, looking from Gemma to Francis, then Sara. Sara still hadn't spoken a single word since I'd come through the door. She was picking at her meatloaf, birdlike, the oddest look on her face.

Before Gemma could answer, Francis was speaking on her behalf (which seriously annoyed me): "On Thursdays, Gemma has a large math packet to do and her online reading assignment. She does that mostly on her own, and she's pretty good about asking me and Sara if there's something she needs help with."

"That's great," I said, not taking my eyes off Gemma. "If I can help with anything, please let me know," I told her.

Gemma nodded. "May I be excused?" she asked, abruptly, dropping her fork beside the plate.

"Yes, you may," Francis spoke before I had the chance. I watched my daughter carry her dish to the kitchen, then I listened to her tiny footsteps going up to her bedroom on the second floor.

"While I have you two alone, I just wanted to say I'm sorry if I misunderstood something today. Sara, you gave me the keys and the directions to school. I thought it was okay to pick up Gemma…"

Sara scooted her chair back loudly. "I did, but I shouldn't have. It was too soon."

"Plus," Francis interrupted again, "Sara said you were very persistent and agitated today, insisting that she look over your discharge papers and accept that you're fit to take back custody of Gemma."

"I did no such thing!" I said, finally losing my temper.

Sara walked off, carrying her plate in one frail, bony hand. I watched her go, feeling even more shocked and hurt. I had half a mind to stand up and grab her wrist, stop her from leaving the room. She was my aunt, my blood— not Francis. If she wouldn't take my side, who would?

"I did bring her the discharge papers," I said, turning back to face Francis. "I forgot to give them to you both when I arrived last night. But I didn't force her to look at them. I didn't try to push her to do anything. She asked me if I could drive, and then she handed over her car keys—"

Francis held up a hand to stop me. "It's okay, Norah. I understand that it was a mistake, on both of your parts. We'll discuss your involvement in Gemma's transportation soon. And I'll look over those papers myself tonight."

Good for you, asshole, that's what I wanted to say.

"Okay, thanks," I mumbled instead. I forced down a few

more bites of meatloaf, before standing up to clear my plate. Francis stared at me, still working slowly on his own heaping pile of food. *What—does he expect me to excuse myself?*

"Thanks for supper," I muttered. In the kitchen, I hoped to find Sara. Maybe if I could just talk to her alone again, then things would seem fine, the way they had earlier when we were together…

But she was nowhere to be found in the kitchen and the sink was full of unwashed plates. Through the library room and foyer, I didn't find her either. Finally, I headed upstairs to my room. It was barely six, but already the sun was dipping low in the sky, a chilly breeze drifting through the open curtains.

Carefully, I made my bed, since I'd forgotten to this morning. Then I took out my suitcase and unloaded the few belongings I had. I tucked my T-shirts and pants into the second drawer, then my handful of underwear and socks in the top. *Might as well get comfortable. If they don't trust me to be alone with my daughter, or even to pick her up from school, they're not going to relinquish control over her until ordered by the court to do so,* I thought, sullenly.

I'd just finished putting away my toiletries and placing my AA book on the bookshelf, when there was a hard knock on my door. I hoped for Gemma but wasn't surprised when I opened up the door to find Francis.

He was holding my coat in his hand. The army-green peacoat looked small and pathetic in his hands. "You left this downstairs at the table."

"Oh. Thank you. I was just finishing unpacking," I said, taking the jacket from him. Another forced smile, another awkward moment with Francis.

"Well, I'll leave you to it then."

I was glad to see him go. I closed the door behind him and listened to his heavy, slow steps going down.

Sighing, I carried my coat over to the empty closet. Again, I tugged at the light, instantaneously remembering that the bulb was out.

"Oh well." I took down one of the wire hangers. It wasn't until I'd hung the coat and closed the closet, that I remembered Jana's card in my pocket. *I'll have to call her and find out exactly which church to go to on Saturday.* But then, I remembered again, my phone was disconnected. *Perhaps Sara or Francis would let me use theirs to make a call...*

But when I reached inside the jacket pocket, Jana's number was gone.

I checked the other pocket, too, just to be sure.

Francis, you asshole, I thought, blood boiling.

Chapter Nine

There are things they don't tell you about getting clean.

For instance, sleep doesn't come easily.

You would think after suffering through withdrawals and getting the drugs out of your system, that your body would eventually return to normal...

Mine never has.

Most nights, I lie in bed for hours, a mixture of physical and mental anguish my only company.

First, there's the restless legs. It usually starts just as I'm dozing off—an electric shock in one leg, sometimes both. As soon as I feel it, I *know*—I'm in for a long night. Tossing and turning, my limbs unable to stay still no matter how hard I try.

The restless legs remind me of those painful nights in rehab, the bone-crushing withdrawals, the shivering/sweating routine...

So, with the restless legs come the memories. Flashes of little things that become big things in my mind. The roiling guilt, the despair… Those can keep me tossing for hours.

And then there's the scars. Mine have healed, but they're still there. The injection sites on my arms and legs, and the hidden ones in between my toes and on my inner thighs—they serve as a constant reminder. At night, they feel enflamed, itching and burning.

My scars actually look worse now than they did when I was using. At least when I was using, the wounds stayed fresh. Now they look like old burn marks, something a veteran of war might carry on his or her skin.

But the memories… those are scars themselves, hidden deep below the skin. Those wounds, they heal. But not for long. Every night they're torn open again, nasty and oozing, never letting me forget.

The worst memory flashes are of being high. They don't tell you this in rehab: the things you thought you forgot aren't actually forgotten. They come back, with a vengeance, and usually when you least expect them. Not just at bedtime either—*all the time*; you can never let your guard down long.

One minute you're standing in the makeup aisle at Rite Aid, picking out a new shade of lipstick. And the next, you catch a whiff of perfume from the guy opening up the case to fetch a bottle for his wife's anniversary gift. The scent tickles your nose, and suddenly you're no longer standing in Rite Aid—you're in the bathroom of your old apartment, squirting on the same perfume in the mirror. Smiling back at yourself with all your teeth. *Damn I smell good*, you think. It seems like a good place to be, back in this memory, getting ready to go out with the man you love. But then that memory leads to what comes next, and you're not in the bathroom of your old apartment sniffing your own damn self; you're high on crystal meth because you couldn't get opioids that day, and you're wandering through your own neighborhood—but it doesn't look like your neighborhood—and you're clutching a knife to your side because you're convinced somebody's trying to kill you.

And that's how you end up running out of Rite Aid, knocking over a carousel of cheap reader glasses, shoving past an old lady in the front door. *Psycho!* someone yells from behind you, but all you want to do is get away... but you can't. You can't escape from your own muddled brain; the memories of things you did that you didn't even realize were memories.

Back in your car in the Rite Aid parking lot, you might feel safe again. But only temporarily. You didn't get the lipstick and you made a fool of yourself, but you're breathing. *You're okay.* You think about how easy it was to be transported back to that awful place—that you-from-before—and then you drive home, having a full-blown panic attack. *What if that happens to me at work? What if I'm driving down the road with my young daughter in the back and I crash because of it? What if what if what if...* and then, maybe I should just stay home and in bed. Because if I'm home and in bed, at least it's only me and the sheets to contend with.

But, as it turns out, the bedroom is just as dangerous.

Thoughts turn wild when the lights go out, my legs jitter and shake, and I crave the sort of sleep I've never been able to obtain.

I closed my eyes in the dark, the scratchy quilt tucked up to my chin. *Please, not tonight,* I pleaded with my legs. But I could already feel the burning in my calves, the uncontrollable urge to move my legs around.

I sat up with a groan, shoving the quilt off the bed.

"Don't look at me like that," I said, getting up. *He's there, even now, in this hellish house. Eyes watching in the dark.*

In the shadowy corner, crouched next to the dresser, was Finn. Not Finn, smiling and happy and healthy Finn. No, not him. *It's Finn the last time I saw him, head half missing... reproachful black eyes in the dark.*

"Not tonight. Not here," I said. I flipped the switch, soft yellow light flooding the bedroom once more.

Finn was gone. My legs were fine. But I was no closer to sleep, that's for sure.

Checking my phone, I saw that it was half past midnight. I needed to be up in less than six hours, to see Gemma off to school. But I knew from my experience in rehab that staying in bed could sometimes make it worse.

I slipped on my coat and shoes. Tucked my vape pen in my pocket. The simple act reminded me of earlier, Jana's card missing from my coat pocket. *Did Francis really search through my pockets and take the card? Or did I simply drop it somewhere?* I wondered.

The house was bitterly cold, even with my coat on.

Gently, I creaked open my bedroom door and poked my head out to the empty hallway. *Silence.*

I needed a glass of water and a quick smoke outside. Perhaps a brief walk in the garden to ease my legs before I tried to lie down again.

I knew Francis wouldn't approve of the vaping or the late-night stroll, but this place wasn't prison, and I needed to get my head on straight before getting back in that bed. My medication helped with anxiety and depression, but as far as the trauma of losing Finn and what I'd gone through with the drugs... *well, that will take time,* my therapist had told me. But: *how long?* No one ever tells you *how long.*

As it turned out, one of the best treatment options for PTSD was this technique called systematic desensitization. To put it in layman's terms, my therapist explained that it meant facing my fears and trauma, bit by bit—exposure therapy—and practicing relaxation techniques. Going for a walk, having a smoke, getting a drink of water—that's how I relaxed. That's how I handled these late-night episodes in rehab.

And that's how I'll deal with them here, Francis be damned.

Damned or not, I still crept like a demented ballerina down the stairs, afraid of being caught out of bed. The wood creaked and groaned under my feet.

When I reached the bottom stairwell, I stopped breathing and listened. The last thing I wanted was to wake up Francis—*I don't need another scolding tonight.*

Lights were out in the foyer and library, coating the heavy wood furniture and shelves in dancing, moonlit shadows. The shadows brought new shapes and dimensions to the room, giving the knick-knacks a sinister glow. Doll eyes watching me as I moved through the room.

I had a brief thought, crazy and sinister, of the doll leaping down from her perch, ceramic legs sliding across the floor…

Relieved to see no one else downstairs, I crept through the library, careful to avoid the doll's stony gaze. A faint glow beamed from the kitchen, a sickly yellow hood light over the stove. I stepped inside and flicked on another light by the sink. The cupboards were full of heavy glass cups. As quietly as I could, I took down a small teacup and filled it with lukewarm sink water. The dinner dishes from earlier were gone, cleaned and whisked away by Sara, I presumed.

If only I could have talked to her earlier, tried to get to the bottom of her fears with Francis. There's no other explanation for why she acts one way when we're alone, and completely different around her husband.

The window above the sink revealed a side view from the house. It was dark out there, low fields stretching endlessly. *That's where I'll sneak off to smoke and walk,* I decided. With Francis and Sara's bedroom on the other side of the house, and Gemma's view from her room upstairs facing the back of the property, no one could see from this side unless they came out to meet me.

I took another sip of water and poured out the rest in the sink. Silently, I slipped back through the library and foyer, and let myself out through the front door.

I closed it softly behind me, double checking to be sure I didn't lock myself out. *That would be bad.*

The wind howled through the trees as I circled around the side of the creepy old house. A flock of birds scattered across the night sky, a few of them swooping so low and close that one of them nearly grazed my cheekbone. *Bats, not birds,* I realized, with a shudder.

Finally, with my back pressed to the bricks, I took several long tokes off my cigarette. Nicotine filled my lungs, the tension in my shoulders and chest instantly contracting. I tried only to hit the e-cig when necessary; and although Francis probably couldn't smell the vapor if I puffed it in my room, I wasn't willing to take any more chances now that I was already on his bad side.

Shivering, I tucked the cig and my hands in my pockets and walked toward the back of the house. For a brief, silly moment I imagined myself in the garden, throwing pebbles at Gemma's back window, sneaking her away from this whole damn place, like I was the knight in shining armor. Her the beautiful princess in her lonely tower.

Francis's stern expression and steely, scolding words came floating back to me... and then I also remembered what that counselor Jana said: *he won't give her back so easily.*

Strolling, I closed my eyes and said a silent prayer—for things to go my way next week in court. After that, I tried to clear my mind of all worries, focusing on blankness, another technique I'd learned from my doctor in rehab.

As I was about to turn back around to go inside, there was a small flash of light moving along the tree line. It was a bright flicker, but then it was gone… *Probably just a firefly*, I thought.

But then I heard the scuffle of footsteps, branches snapping in the dark. I moved to the side of the house again, pressing myself against the bricks, breathlessly. I tried to make myself small in the shadow below the stone-grey awning.

Eyes skimming the tree line, I wondered if I'd imagined the flash of light and the branches…

But then the light reappeared, a small dull glow of a torch, bouncing back and forth, moving toward me through the trees. Then a low cough. *A man's cough.*

Someone is out there in the forest, coming toward the house! My body bucked, ready to make a run for it back inside. But then, it was too late; a shadowy figured emerged from between two trees. With my eyes focused on him, I could see now what I had missed—there was a barely noticeable dirt path leading into the woods. And Uncle Francis was coming out of it.

What the hell is he doing out there in the forest so late?

As a second figure emerged beside him, I held in a gasp. They stopped, right at the edge of the pathway, their bodies blue-black shapes in the moonlit gap between trees and land.

Aunt Sara? I wondered.

But it wasn't Sara. There was something youthful in the woman's movements. She leaned in close to Francis. Their heads were practically pressed together; I could hear them talking. Low murmurs, too quiet to hear. From where I was standing, I had a clear side profile of Francis, but the woman was deeper in the shadows of the trees. All I could see was how they stood, and I could make out the petite curves of her body and the bouncy short bob she wore her hair in.

Francis's lover, perhaps?

I felt a flash of anger. Sorrow for Aunt Sara. Francis moved and the woman did too. For a second, I caught a flash of her face. She was a stranger to me.

But then there was something else too… a thought.

I reached for my phone in my back pocket. *Maybe if I could snap a quick picture, I could use this to convince Francis to let me leave — quietly, lips sealed — with my daughter.*

But that was a nasty thought. A selfish thought. Using Sara's pain to my own advantage.

Maybe I'll just take a pic and show Aunt Sara. Maybe she won't be so loyal to her domineering husband if she learns about his late-night rendezvous with this bouncy forest creature…

I lifted my phone, thumb fumbling to open the camera app—and then Francis was walking. They were coming toward me, heading straight for the side of the house!

I turned, speed-walking around the corner, darting back up the porch steps. I'd barely made it inside and closed the door behind me when I heard the sound of his heavy boots on the porch.

Oh no! Did he see me spying?

I raced through the library and up the steps to my room, reaching the top of the staircase with a huff just as the front door creaked open. From the top of the stairs, in the dark cover of the lightless hallway, I watched as Uncle Francis returned. He was alone. He didn't open the door all the way, shimmying his way inside and nudging the door shut behind him. *Slithering like a snake. A snake with something to hide.*

Disgusted, I watched as my uncle tiptoed through the library, then disappeared down the hallway to the room he shared with Aunt Sara.

So, he's sneaking around with another woman. Damn, I should have tried to get a picture sooner, while they were standing face to face, the very moment I saw them...

I was afraid to move from my perch at the top of the stairs; afraid Francis might realize I was awake if he heard my footsteps overhead. I slid down the wall in the hallway, knees tucked close to my chest. I waited in the dark, considering what I'd just seen.

Who was the woman? And what were they doing out there? Francis, with his silent judgment and self-righteous attitude, hardly seemed the type to have an affair. And he certainly wasn't what I'd consider a 'catch', not for a pretty young woman like that...

I sat in the hallway for what felt like an hour before finally retreating to my room.

Shivering, I crawled beneath the covers. Wondering again if I should tell Aunt Sara.

It could have been perfectly harmless. A friend, a neighbor... hell, it could have been his sister. The other day,

I hadn't met Susie's mother, Merrill. It could have been her...

I thought I'd never fall asleep, with my heart thumping in my chest and my thoughts racing endlessly, but within minutes of crawling back into bed, I fell into a deep, dreamless sleep.

Chapter Ten

STEP 6: ACCEPTANCE

My phone alarm shook me awake at six on the dot, the melancholy voice of Kurt Cobain singing 'I Just Want to Sleep'. It was a setting I'd used for waking up for nearly two years now. *Probably time to change it.*

Usually, I liked to lie on my cot in rehab for a few minutes, listening to the lyrics until one of my bunk mates gave me an irritated shake.

But today, I was right out of bed, despite the fact that I'd slept less than five hours. Tugging on khakis and a thin button-down shirt that had seen better days, I remembered the strange events of last night.

My late-night stroll, and Francis out there at the edge of the woods with a strange woman, whispering in the dark.

Somehow, it seemed less strange in the light of day. *It's not my business who he's meeting at night, just like it's not my business if he's faithful to Sara or not.*

My only focus is Gemma.

In the bathroom, I washed my face and brushed my teeth. I pulled my hair back into a loose ponytail, then changed my mind and combed it straight, needling out the tangles.

Gemma left for school at 6.30, according to Sara. Today I wanted to see her off and make a good impression on Francis. I need to show him that I was trustworthy, so that he would let me resume my own responsibilities with my daughter.

At 6.12, I descended the steps peppily, eager to make some toast and jam for my daughter like I used to when she attended preschool.

But the house felt eerily still.

"Hello?"

Thinking they might have overslept, I climbed Gemma's stairs, two at a time. "You up, Gemma?" I called.

But her bed was empty, last night's pajamas still curled on the floor. *Damn. How did I miss them again?*

"What are you doing up here?"

Gasping, I turned to find Aunt Sara, leaning in the doorway. She looked weary.

What do you think I'm doing? I wanted to scream.

"I wanted to make sure Gemma didn't oversleep for school. You said they left at 6.30 on school days…"

"I did?" Aunt Sara rubbed her cheeks with both hands, looking confused. "I'm sorry, dear. I must have been mistaken. They get up at 5.30 and leave a few minutes after six each day…"

I thought about the other day—the 2.35 pick-up time that was off by more than a half hour.

Is my aunt trying to confuse me, or is she confused herself? I wondered.

Based on the bewildered look on her face, I had to assume the latter.

"It's okay, Aunt Sara," I sighed. "Would you like me to fix you some breakfast?"

"A cup of coffee would be great. It's Thursday, isn't it?"

Concern rising, I said, "Yes, it is."

"Ah, that's right. I volunteer at the school on Thursdays and Fridays. Making copies, sorting books in the school library, some janitorial stuff. Anything they need me to do, that's what I do."

This was news to me. "That's wonderful. I had no idea you volunteered. You used to teach, didn't you? Were you a teacher at Restoration?"

Sara nodded, then bent down to pluck up Gemma's soiled laundry. "That's right. I loved it, but I was ready to go when I did. But, now that I'm older, it's nice to give back. And since Gemma goes to school there, I thought it would be nice to volunteer and perhaps run into her at school."

She won't be going there long. But I kept that thought to myself.

"How nice! Do you need me to drive you?" I offered.

Sara's eyes narrowed. "I'm a little forgetful, not senile. I can drive just fine."

My cheeks flushed. "I know that. I was just trying to be nice. You all have done so much to help out me and

Gemma, I just thought…" It was true, I realized. More than anything, I wanted to feel useful. And so far, since arriving here, I'd felt far from it.

"I'm sorry, dear." Sara reached out, touching my elbow. "I don't need a ride, but I would love that coffee… I need to shower and get dressed. I'm supposed to be there at 7.15."

"Sure." I followed Sara back down the windy steps, pacing myself behind her. She was slow, thin hands spotted with age gripping the handrail for dear life. Until now, I hadn't realized how frail she seemed; and the confusion was a surprise. *Perhaps the entire miscommunication yesterday was a result of Sara's confusion*, I considered.

"The layout of this home is interesting. I wonder why the two different floors are disconnected?" I said, as Sara reached the landing.

"Oh, you don't know, do you? This place, in addition to being a farm, also used to be a nunnery."

"A nunnery?" I asked, unable to hide my surprise. "How old is this place?"

"More than a century old, my dear. It's been in Francis's family for generations. His great-great-grandmother trained to be a nun here. She eventually bought the place and became the Mother Superior. She had hoped it would remain a nunnery, but as you can see, her descendants were less prone to religion." She smiled.

"That's… incredible," I said, seeing the place in a whole new light. We made our way toward the kitchen.

Sara took a seat on a stool at the kitchen island and directed me, step by step, on how to operate her complicated espresso machine. It seemed like an odd item for an elderly, old-fashioned couple to possess. But who I was to judge? And for someone prone to confusion, she sure knew how she liked her coffee.

"But why the two separate floors?" I added a splash of milk and sugar to both of our cups. I placed hers on a saucer and set it carefully in front of her, careful not to dump it on her lap with my shaky hands. I'd come downstairs in a rush, forgetting my morning medication. *Must take that as soon as Sara leaves for her volunteer work*, I mentally noted.

"Ah. Because it wasn't really a nunnery. It was more of what they called a priory back then, because both men and women lived here, and they earned their keep by working the fertile land. The men were on one side of the house, the women on the other. With their vows of chastity, I guess they couldn't take any chances," Sara chuckled.

"I suppose they couldn't trust them to make their own good choices," I said, a slight trace of bitterness in my tone.

Sara blew steam from the top of her coffee, eyes meeting mine. "Well, to be honest, some of the women who came here were troubled. And I don't know this for certain, but I'm pretty sure that some came against their will."

I raised my eyebrows. "So, they were held here like prisoners?"

Sara rolled her eyes. "No, of course not. Francis's great-great-grandmother, Rosemary, was many things. But she was never cruel." I fought the urge to point out the facts—that there was no chance in hell Sara or Francis met this great-great Rosemary at the turn of the century. Unless she was some sort of time traveler.

"The women were... How do I put it? Some of them were cast aside by their family. They had nowhere else to go. The black sheep, you might call them. Some were here as an ultimatum, their last chance to win their way back into their family's good graces. And many were prone to sin... sex, drugs, you name it."

I frowned, thinking about my own predicament.

"That's sad," I said, taking a sip of my coffee. It was bitter-tasting and piping hot and I had to spit it back in the cup.

"For many, it was a godsend," Sara said, defensively.

"And what about the men who were here? Were they cast-outs and sinners, too?" I asked, smirking.

"Who knows?" Sara shrugged. She stood, carried her half-empty cup to the sink, and started washing.

Who knows? I thought about all of the men in my life, particularly Allen, Gemma's biological father whom she had never met.

Allen with his big dreams and his academic scholarship. Allen with his *plans*.

No one was surprised when he left me; when he went on to college, carrying on with his life as though nothing had ever happened. *Like a baby hadn't been born.*

And if they did mention Allen's behavior, it was to give excuses. *He was only seventeen. He had a bright future. What did you expect? Most boys his age would have done the same.*

But if the shoe were on the other foot... *oh, how the town would have talked.* If I'd have dumped Gemma off on Allen's doorstep and went on my merry way to college, following all my big *plans* and *dreams*... that would have been another story.

The moment we become mothers, we start disappearing.

It's no longer about us, it's about these tiny people, these tiny extensions of *us*. Everything we do is viewed through the lens of *mother*.

How could you do that to your kid? the quiet single lady who sat in the corner at group used to ask me. *When I become a mother, I'll never do anything to fuck it up,* she had told me, angrily.

I loved most of my fellow group members, but some less than others. Even though we were all there for the same reason, we weren't above being judgmental to each other. *I'd never shoot up. I'm glad I never took it that far,* one man said, when I showed them my track marks. And just the mere mention of my having a daughter... It quickly made me a villain.

Because no decent mother would do that. Fathers, yeah. But not mothers... We are meant to be perfect.

We are meant to disappear as individuals when we assume our new role.

Every part of who of I was faded away when Gemma was born. My friends and my hobbies. My looks.

Men sowing their oats is normal. Men choosing themselves over children is not only normal but *expected* most of the time.

When women do it it's disgraceful.

Simply put: it's *unforgivable.*

"You okay? Looking a little foggy-eyed like me." Sara grinned.

I cleared my throat, thinking about the women who used to live here. Trapped in a place they didn't want to be, feeling judged for their "sins", just like me. Like them, I'd have to prove myself if I wanted to get away from this shit.

"I'm fine."

"Well, good. I'll go get ready then. I need to head out in the next twenty minutes."

"Okay, Sara," I said, absentmindedly.

As she went to get ready, I wiped down the kitchen counters with a rag and Lysol. Then I washed and put away the remaining dishes.

Doing chores to earn my keep.

Chapter Eleven

W ith no car and nothing within walking distance, I had no choice but to spend my day at the creepy old house.

I started out my day in the bedroom, making my bed. Getting the corners precise, the way I learned to in rehab. After, I dusted the bookshelf, then I mopped the tub and floor in the bathroom.

Then I selected a couple of romance novels from the shelf in the library, setting them aside for later tonight. *I need a healthy distraction.*

The thought of lying about all day, getting lost in a good story, sounded pretty good to me.

But I hadn't read romance since losing Finn, and the thought of reading love scenes, or even sex scenes that reminded me... I put the novels back and picked up a soft-backed thriller with a ghostly girl on the cover.

Slowly, I moved room to room with my rag, swiping

dressers and baseboards for dust. As I moved through the dark-paneled corridors and chilly rooms, I couldn't help thinking about the women—and men—who had once lived here. *I wonder who stayed in my room? Another troubled girl, like me, perhaps? Forced to grovel her way back into society's good graces?*

The downstairs bathroom was neat, minus a few patches of mildew on the ceiling. I wiped down the sink and commode for good measure, then returned upstairs to the playroom. I'd barely been inside it since that first day when Gemma and Susie were playing, and I assumed that a toy room, of all places, could use a little sprucing up.

The floor, riddled with toys and books and blocks, brought a soft smile to my face. *At least Gemma has been having some fun while I was away.*

At home, we didn't have the luxury of having excess toys, even if we could afford them. We kept two small toy chests at the foot of Gemma's bed and when she grew tired of certain dolls or games, we would drop them off at the charity center.

I scooped up blocks and Lincoln Logs, dumping them into a long plastic toy bin along the wall. There was a gang of Barbies sitting in a circle, prim points of their toes touching as though they'd been deep in conversation before I arrived.

Again, my face lit up with a smile, thinking of Gemma playing. She had always loved playing, especially on our own, and she had a big imagination. Sometimes, particularly when she was a toddler, I would just sit and watch her. Always in her own world, making up stories—one day, a ballerina competing for her crown. The next, she was an astronaut on planet Jupiter, searching for signs of extraterrestrial life as she scooted along the floor with a plastic toy magnifying glass.

I left the Barbies where they were, instead organizing a stack of board games into one corner and lining up stuffed animals and books on a low-lying, built-in shelf on the south-facing wall.

Wiping my brow, I stood and stretched. It felt like a hundred degrees suddenly. The playroom was large but there were no windows and no ceiling fans. Just a little toy-filled cave.

A wave of dizziness rolled through me, and I sat down on the carpet next to Gemma's doll-gang, closing my eyes momentarily.

I forgot to eat breakfast this morning, I remembered. That was one good thing about the rehab center—*routine*. I stood slowly, leaving my dust rag on the floor where it lay. The cleaning could wait until later—I needed a quick bite to eat.

I also need to take my medicine, I thought, wearily, heading out the door of the playroom.

I turned back, suddenly, just remembering to flip out the light—and that's when I saw it.

Strange lines in the flowery wallpaper behind the bookshelf. Something out of place. Unusual.

Perhaps it was a sixth sense, or some sort of leftover Nancy Drew-esque fantasy from my youth, but I moved to the shelf to get a closer look.

"I'll be damned." I slid my fingers along the line. It was the outline of some sort of door.

But the shelf was blocking the rest of it.

Impulsively, I began sliding the boardgames and books off the shelves. Then I inched the heavy wooden shelf forward, grunting as I tried to scoot it.

I'd barely moved it a few inches; just enough to sneak my arm farther inside. Pressing my cheek against the wall and straining my arm, I tried to see or feel what lay behind the shelf.

"Whoa."

It was a small door, covered in the same old-fashioned wallpaper as the rest of the room.

My fingers slid down, connecting with a tiny gold knob in its center.

Sweat was beading on my upper lip and forehead and dampening the front of my long-sleeved shirt. Groaning, I scraped my arm as I yanked on the shelf, trying to pull it forward a bit.

Impulsively, I tugged my sweaty top over my head and loosened my bra, then crossed the hallway toward my own room.

Changing into shorts and a thin tank top, I returned to the shelf, body buzzing with a strange sort of excitement.

Reminding myself to bend at the knees, so as not to hurt my back, I lifted the right side of the shelf as much as possible and thrust it forward a good five inches this time.

Just enough to reach the knob.

This time, I was able to turn it, much to my delight.

Every part of my being expected the door to be locked, or perhaps not to be a real door after all, just a childish illusion… but then it rotated easily in my hand. I tried to pull the door forward from the wall, and instantly realized my mistake. The door was meant to swing inward, not out.

This time when I turned the knob, I used my other hand to give the door a sturdy push.

There was a small sucking sound, like a long overdue exhale of breath as the door opened. A thick cloud of dust tickled my nose and made my eyes water.

Sucking in my gut, I slid behind the bookshelf and ducked inside the tiny door.

Chapter Twelve

I couldn't believe my eyes. *This can't be real,* I thought, my phone torch held out in front of me like a glowing shield.

But it *was* real—through the stooped doorway was a long dark passageway.

Hands shaking, I nearly dropped my phone as I fumbled around, trying to increase the brightness of my torch.

The battery was sitting at 27 percent, not nearly enough power. I considered turning back, going to search for a bonafide flashlight downstairs, but I found myself edging further along the narrow hallway, pulled by the allure of the mysteries ahead.

I took a few measured steps, listening—for what, exactly? I wasn't sure.

Swinging the beam side to side, I was shocked to find the same flowery wallpaper of the playroom lining either side of the hall. I'd expected an unfinished portion of the house, perhaps a crawlspace or unkept room that was meant to be added on but never was.

But despite the icy cold darkness and vacuum-sealed bubble of silence, this seemed to be a part of the house that was once in use. *Who closed it off, and why?* I wondered.

At the end of the hallway, my heart fluttered at the next discovery. A dark wood staircase wound all the way around like a corkscrew into a gloomy square opening above. Before I could change my mind, I was climbing, shining the light overhead. Checking for spiders, or worse.

My mouth fell open as I reached the top stair. A small, round-shaped space—the sweet room of a little girl. The wallpaper was covered in dainty rosebuds; the soft duvet on the bed rosy and red to match it. Delicate furniture—a miniature bookshelf, classic Golden books on its shelves, and the remnants of a forgotten dollhouse in the corner. The only thing that wasn't childlike in the room was a stiff metal desk. A miniature window was featured above the desk, like a tiny rain hole, or a port hole in a boat.

I leaned over the desk, looking out, wearily. The silly child in me almost imagined a portal to another world, a window to a forgotten era. But, instead, I had a cloudy, limited view of the back garden. *Funny how I never noticed the miniature window up here while I was out there.*

I glanced at the desk, at a small stash of yellowing photos that were spread wide like a fan at its center.

Taking a seat in the stiff chair, I used my light to pore over the images on the desk. Some of the photos were older than others, black and white images of the house itself, at different stages.

In one photo, a stern-faced family of five stood on the stoop of a porch; I recognized it as the front porchway of my aunt and uncle's home, but this was a time when it was newer, less crumbly. A flash of better days.

In another photo, there was a row of women dressed like nuns—but they were so young, less women than girls. The hideous house formed the backdrop of the photo, although something was missing. *No gargoyles yet*, I realized.

I moved back to the image of the family. This one looked old, yet less grainy than the one with the nuns. As I peered into the faces of the children who stood between what I could only assume was the mother and father, I thought I recognized one of them. A young boy and two older sisters, close enough in appearance that they must be siblings. I was certain the boy was Francis. *This is his family's home*, I remembered Sara telling me.

Shivering, I put the two photos back on the desk and examined the other three. These were clearly newer, as they were Polaroids and in color. In all three there was only one subject—a young girl with cherry-red hair and cerulean eyes. The picture seemed old and new, perhaps only twenty years old or so. I looked at the images of the strange young girl. All shot outside, and close to the brow.

She was familiar, that smile. Those dimples in her cheeks... *Could this be my mother when she was younger?*

But that was ridiculous; my mother's hair had been dark like mine and Aunt Sara's. And, although I'd seen very few photos of my mother as a young girl, I had seen some—and I knew this girl wasn't her.

Two of the photos of the girl were blank on the back, but the third one was not.

Constance, age five.

I knew no one named Constance in our family, but that didn't mean much, truly. My mom and Aunt Sara had more family on their side that I hadn't met, distant relatives who lived farther west. And I knew absolutely nothing about Francis's family. *This could be his sister as a child, the one I've never met. Or perhaps a niece or cousin?* There was no way to know for sure.

But the familiarity of the girl filled me with a strange sense of nostalgia.

Looking closer, I noticed that the background of each photo was blurry, as though the girl was caught mid-flight, always moving. In this one, she was darting playfully through the grass. In another, arms outstretched, her head was half turned, as though someone had tried to take a photo of her spinning in circles.

The girl looked happy. Carefree. And no matter how hard I tried, I couldn't shake the thought: *I know her.*

I closed my eyes and when I did, I could almost see her there—darting through the bushes, hiding behind statues. Her giggle, sweet sounds of a ringing bell.

I know her. I played with her as a child here. I know I did.

And this room—*this isn't the first time I've been inside it.* Although, when I had visited before, I didn't think it was walled off and hidden…

Back down the curved staircase, I shone my light, examining more of the closed-off hallway behind the wall. *Why did they close this area off, and especially the beautiful loft room on the third floor?* This hallway had obviously been part of the second floor, originally, and the stairs were easy access to the third-floor bedroom.

I considered the fact that this portion of the home might be structurally unsafe. *For my sake, I hope that's not the reason why.* I imagined, ever so briefly, what I would do if the ceiling or walls closed in on me; I'd be stuck in the interior walls of my aunt's home, unable to breathe or cry for help…

Stop. Don't think things like that that, I chastised myself. I'd always been that sort of person—doom and gloom. *Perhaps that's what drew me to the drugs, and Finn's dark side, to begin with.*

Suddenly, I remembered the thudding noises above my room. Could those have been coming from the third-floor bedroom? *Perhaps there are rats up there,* I thought with a shudder. But I hadn't seen anything to indicate that while I was up there.

I was about to give up with exploring the hallway when I saw it—a trapdoor in the floor at the southernmost tip of the passage. *Wow. This place keeps getting weirder.*

As I squatted for a closer look, I was surprised to find a recessed ring-pull made of antique brass on the door.

Well, I've come this far. Why stop now?

I tugged on the brass ring, grunting as the thick door groaned open before me. For the second time today, I shone my phone torch into a dark hole, waiting to see what leapt out from inside it.

But, once again, I was met with a strange narrow passageway. Another closed off interior passage—*with another child's room, perhaps?*

This time, the passage was longer and narrower, no secret stairwells above. But what I found at the end of it was more surprising. A trapdoor, identical to the first, but this time, I found light on the other end.

I was standing in my daughter's bedroom on the other side of the house.

Chapter Thirteen

My mind was spinning, trying to wrap itself around the maze I'd just come out of.

There was a hidden entrance in the playroom that connected both wings of the house. And another, unused bedroom, on the third floor, that used to belong to a child. *A child I may, or may not, remember from my own childhood.*

I wondered why my aunt and uncle had blocked off the hallway that connected the second floor. For a moment, it crossed my mind that perhaps I was the reason. *Did they block it off before I came to ensure I had fewer ways to access Gemma?*

But, for some reason, I didn't quite buy that theory. *It looks like it's been closed off for years.*

I was about to retrace my steps, go back through Gemma's closet to get to my side, when I heard a loud thudding sound below.

Oh God! Someone's home!

Panicked, and not knowing why, I raced down the stairs and through the kitchen, to see what was going on. *Someone's knocking,* I realized.

At least it's not Francis unless he forgot his house key. The last thing I need is another run-in with him when he's pissed, I thought.

The knocking grew louder still as I raced through the sitting room, unlatched the lock, and threw the front door open. It was only then that I realized how I must look; sweaty and breathless, my shirt and shorts coated in dust from sliding behind the shelving and through the dusty, closed-off hallways.

"Hello," said the stranger on the front porch. She looked me up and down wearily as I caught my breath. "I'm Merrill. You must be Norah." She spat out my name as though it tasted funny in her mouth.

Merrill. Francis's sister, I recalled. I thought about that call the other day, the one between her and Aunt Sara. The conversation about me, doubting my sobriety.

"Yep. That's me. Come on in." Although unsure why she was visiting during the day when Francis and Sara weren't home, I motioned her to come inside.

She made a beeline for the kitchen and I followed, taking the opportunity to dust off my shoulders and fan out my sweaty tank top.

"Sorry it took me so long to come to the door. I was upstairs cleaning and didn't hear you at first. Francis and Sara aren't in right now."

"Uh-huh." Merrill placed her bulky handbag on the

kitchen counter and started opening and closing the bottom cupboards.

"Can I help you find something?" A silly thing to say, considering I didn't know my way around the kitchen much yet.

"Bingo," Merrill said, lifting a heavy ceramic pie dish from the bottom shelf. "I let Sara borrow this a while back."

"Oh, okay. Sara's a great cook," I said, awkwardly, leaning my hip against the kitchen island. Now that Merrill was standing still, and facing me, I could see the resemblance to Francis. They were both tall and broad-shouldered with that square jaw, although Merrill was more feminine, soft brown curls cascading down her back.

"She is a great cook," Merrill said, still gripping the dish in her hand. She looked around the kitchen, eyes eventually resting back on me. "What were you cleaning, exactly? You look a little scattered."

My stomach curled with unease. Like Francis, I could see that disapproving look in her eye.

"The upstairs bathroom and playroom. Oh, I met your daughter, Susie, the other day. What a sweet kid," I said, trying out a nervous smile.

"She is. She adores Gemma. I'd love to get them together again soon, maybe for a sleepover."

"I'm sure Gemma would love that," I said, honestly.

"She's happy here, you know."

For a moment, it took me a minute to realize she was referring to Gemma.

"Yes," I said, steadily, although my mind was circling

back to that letter, the one she wrote me in rehab. "I'm grateful to Sara and Francis for taking care of her while I couldn't..."

"They're great people. Very responsible and loving." *Unlike you, the drug addict mother*, I filled in for her, reading her unsaid words like a book.

As much as I wanted to agree with her, I was reaching my fill on niceties.

"Is there anything else you need? I'm going to head back up and finish scrubbing the tub," I lied, standing straighter.

"No, I'll just take this. Tell Sara I stopped by when she returns." Merrill shifted the heavy dishware in her hands. *She certainly isn't the woman I saw Francis talking to last night.* Even though I hadn't seen the woman's face too clearly, she was small and petite, nothing like Merrill.

I walked her to the door, eager for Francis's female clone to move on. "It was nice to meet you, Merrill," I told her. *Another lie.*

At the doorway, she stopped, turning back to me with a stern look etched on her miserable face. "My brother is a good man, Norah. Better than most. I can't pretend to know why he's letting you stay here even though the custody hearing hasn't happened yet. Just don't take advantage of his generosity. Or Sara's."

Generosity. Is that what you call it? Because it stopped feeling like "generosity" on my second day here.

Speechless, I watched Merrill turn and go, not bothering to defend myself.

Chapter Fourteen

That night, when Gemma and my aunt and uncle returned, I didn't mention Merrill's visit. I certainly didn't mention my discovery in the playroom, or my exploration of the strange child's bedroom and the connecting hallway to Gemma.

I'd been careful to cover my tracks, double checking I'd closed the trapdoors, and securing the door and shelf in the playroom as soon as Merrill had gone.

"How was your day?" Francis boomed, as though he could read my mind from across the table. We were having spaghetti and meatballs, usually a favorite of mine. But the noodles were too hard, the sauce oily and thick on my tongue.

"It was good. I did a little cleaning and spent some time reading the *Big Book*." The second part was a lie. I promised myself that I'd work on the steps tonight before I went to bed. I wasn't having any cravings, not really, but I couldn't afford to let myself slide when it came to my sobriety. Especially not now, when I was so close to being fully reunited with my daughter.

"Hmm," Francis said, through a mouthful of meatballs. I wondered if Merrill had told him about today—me, sweaty and disheveled at the door.

My stomach turned, and I shifted my focus to Gemma.

"How about you, sweetheart? What did you do at school?"

Gemma, too, was picking at her food. "Not much," she said.

Before I could ask her more, Sara was clearing off our plates and shuffling Gemma down the hall for her shower.

Later, I was permitted—with Francis standing over me, of course—to tuck Gemma in and read her a bedtime story. She had requested a colorful book called *A Bad Case of the Stripes*. A strange story about a girl who wakes up to find herself covered in stripes, it was part comedy, part horror, in my opinion. But the ending came with a great message, about learning to love and accept yourself in your own skin. *Oh, if only real-life stories always had a good and meaningful ending like this one*, I thought, smiling sleepily at my daughter.

Gemma's eyes were growing heavy with sleep. I kissed them, remembering how tired she used to get back in the apartment when I read to her. Sometimes, we would read on the sofa and she'd fall asleep so fast that I had to carry her to bed. The older she became, the harder it was to lift her. I never thought I'd miss holding a kid in my arms.

Those early baby days, my forearms and biceps would ache from all the heavy lifting and the massive car seat she rode in.

I noticed another book sitting on her bedside table. Roald Dahl's *The Witches*. She had a bookmark plugged in the center of it.

"You reading that one now?" I said, pointing at it.

Gemma came awake, raising up to her elbows. "It's completely terrifying, but I love it."

I loved seeing the way her face came to life when she talked about reading and stories. It reminded me of myself at her age.

"That was one of my favorites as a kid, too," I said, tapping the end of her nose with my pointer finger. "Okay. Lay back again. It's time to get some sleep." I leaned over and kissed her on the forehead.

"Night, Mom."

Francis, who had remained quiet during our story time, was still silent as we walked back downstairs together. For a moment, I had this irrational thought—that somehow he knew what I'd done today, exploring the hidden halls of his creepy family home.

Back in the kitchen, I poured a glass of milk and offered one to Francis. He shook his head, bending down in front of the sink. Reaching in the cabinet below, he took out a couple of mousetraps.

"I thought I heard some mice the other night, too," I said, wiping off my mouth with the back of my hand.

"Yeah," he said, staring down at the traps, eyes lost in thought.

As I finished my milk, I could feel him, eyes studying me in the low-lit kitchen. There was something curious in his gaze this time, not judgmental, which was his go-to look, but something else. I was certain he was going to say something, or ask me a question, but then he simply wished me goodnight and disappeared to his room with Sara, carrying his mousetraps in tow.

Such a strange man, I thought. I smiled as I remembered the scene in *The Witches* when a boy was transformed into a mouse. *Oh, how I'd love to do that to Francis sometime*, I thought.

Every part of me had wanted to ask him—"Who's that woman you've been sneaking around with outside at night?" Just to see the look on his face.

When I heard the heavy door to their bedroom close, I tiptoed over to the sink and placed my empty milk glass inside it. Then, I moved quickly, opening up the cabinet under the sink to snatch up the Maglite I'd spotted earlier.

———

Unable to sleep, I lay awake in bed, legs jittery in the dark. The only consolation was that tonight my thoughts weren't whirling with memories of Finn, or intrusive flashes of finding him dead. Instead, I was thinking about Constance, trying to remember a little girl from my youth on my few visits to see my aunt. I'd thought it was Mom and I, playing in the garden in my memories... but perhaps it was the girl who lived here. A child belonging to Sara and Francis, perhaps one who died?

I shuddered. Lord, I hoped not. As frustrated as I was with my aunt and uncle, the thought of them experiencing the loss of a child—well, that was too much to bear. Hard enough to lose a partner you love, but a child? I couldn't wrap my brain around that sort of pain. And I didn't want to.

Glancing at my phone, I was surprised to find it was half past midnight again. The house was eerily quiet and would probably stay that way for the remainder of the night. *If you're going, you might as well do it now.*

I counted to ten and then I stood, reaching for the heavy Maglite I'd hidden under the covers earlier. I wanted to explore the passage more, see if I could find out more about Francis and Sara. *If they're hiding something, I want to know what it is—after all, my daughter is basically being held here while custody is pending.*

I took my time, moving slowly through the playroom. While the house was filled with sound before bedtime, I'd scooted the bookcase out just far enough so I could slip inside fairly soundlessly.

Again, I was greeted with the thick smell of dust and something rotten as I entered the hallway entrance behind the bookcase. Although, this time, I had the bright white light of the flashlight to help guide me.

I moved slowly back and forth through the hallway, looking for anything I'd missed earlier. Nothing besides the door leading to Gemma's hallway and the third-floor room above.

I took my time on the stairs, so afraid any creak or moan would wake up Francis or Sara. But the stairs were eerily silent this time, and as I popped my head into the loft room above, I held my breath—waiting to meet with a ghost or something worse.

The room was scarier in the dark of night, the flashlight casting sinister shadows on the rosebud walls. But there was nothing and no one to be afraid of up here.

Gently, I lifted the mattress on the bed and bent down to look inside the dollhouse. There were no hidden secrets under the bed, and the dollhouse looked like the typical toy house of a little girl—dark-haired doll lying still on its bed, little bitty wooden pieces of furniture. I touched a miniature table, picked up one of the tiny chairs and inspected it.

I was hit with a memory—me, right here in this same place, sitting on my knees. Playing with another girl. Playing house.

I was just putting the doll chair back in its place, when I heard a soft thud, felt the vibration of a door closing downstairs. Frozen in place, I held my breath. Waiting. *But waiting for what?*

I listened for the sound of footsteps on the stairs, someone coming up to catch me in this hidden room… but there was nothing.

Finally, able to breathe again, I processed the sound. It was the door, someone going in or out downstairs, I realized.

Perhaps Francis, having another secret rendezvous? *I sure hope so. If he is, I want to catch him and find out what he's really up to.*

I got to my feet and moved to the circular window. I pressed my face to the tiny porthole window. Blinked.

At first, all I could see was my own moon-white reflection peering back at me in the glass. But then my eyes adjusted. There was a full moon in the sky, the back garden illuminated by its shadow.

And much to my chagrin, I spotted my uncle once again, sneaking around in the dark of night.

Chapter Fifteen

M y uncle hovered like a spider, silent and waiting, in
the shadowy gap between the Belladonna statue
and the koi pond.

I moved through the shadows, creeping through the
hallway and floating soundlessly down the wooden
staircase.

I can be a spider too.

Thoughts racing, my heart pummeling my chest like a
manic drum, I held my breath and slid the front door open.
My mind was already circling, creating excuses for why I
was outside this late if he caught me...

You're going to get caught. It's inevitable.

I shut the door behind me, praying Sara was sound
asleep in her room. *If she doesn't hear Francis sneaking around
at night, then she won't hear me either... Right?*

The front porch steps creaked underfoot, and a chilly
bite in the August air sucked the breath right from my

chest. Body buzzing with adrenaline, I circled the house, and walked on the tips of my toes until I had reached the end of the shadowy awning, unable to go any farther without stepping out and revealing myself.

Taking a deep breath, I swallowed my fears and peeked my head around the corner to look at the backside of the property.

The garden was bathed in moonlight, wet and gleaming like a wild jungle from a hazy, midnight-summer dream.

As suspected, Francis was gone from his slippery spot in the shadows. *He's probably deep in the woods by now… probably meeting with his secret lover again. But is she his lover… or something else? I don't trust him, not in the slightest. And how can I trust my child with these people, with their strange rules and midnight ramblings…?*

I only hoped that I hadn't given him too much of a head start. My cell phone was in my pocket, silent mode engaged. I slid it out, gripping it forcefully in my hand, as I willed my feet to move forward in the dark. Like a lion stalking its prey, I crept soundlessly—or at least I tried to— and I slipped through the hedges, crossing through the same dark shadows I'd spotted him in only moments earlier from the attic window.

Light granted by tonight's full moon served as my guide, as I followed the path toward the forest. It emerged between two trees like a skinny moon-white mouth beckoning me to enter its evil underbelly.

The thought of Francis waiting somewhere, tucked

between the hedges and trees, waiting to... *what? Pounce and get me?*

I shook away those thoughts. *He's the one acting strange, creeping around outside in the dark, meeting women while my aunt is sleeping. Sure, following him is a bit strange too, but I must protect my daughter. And if I can find out something to use as leverage, perhaps that will help him see things my way...*

The path grew narrower; quietly, I swatted at sharp branches, trying to avoid rocks and twigs with my thin-soled tennis shoes. Finally, I didn't have to worry too much about sound, because the forest was alive with the sounds of summer: tree frogs croaking, crickets chirping, the lonely hoot of an owl from somewhere in the canopy of trees above.

As the end of the path grew nearer, I snaked off-course, creeping through brush and trees. I could see a shed, one solitary light glowing through a small glass window with a cracked pane. *What is my uncle doing out there? Having a meet-up in that eerie old outbuilding? How romantic!*

Right on cue, I heard the heavy slamming of doors and a low grunt. I let out an involuntary gasp, stepping back into the shadowy underbrush along the tree line. *I have to move closer.*

But I couldn't move forward, exposing myself, until I figured out where he was at, exactly. An then it came: an answer to my prayers. A soft light in the dark, circular and low-lit... My uncle moved around by the shed, carrying a small torchlight by his side. He was alone. *But where's the woman?*

I held my breath as I watched him.

Francis cleared his throat and shuffled over to a rusted-out truck parked behind the shed, the front end sticking out, moonlight glinting off the busted headlights. There was a heavy clank, as though he were dropping the tailgate, but I couldn't see him anymore once he was behind the shed.

I watched and waited, heart full of disappointment. *What am I doing out here, wasting my time?* I wondered. Suddenly, my uncle reappeared, carrying what looked like some sort of metal tool in his hand.

So, he's out here working tonight in the shed — not meeting up with his mistress or doing anything criminal or suspicious after all.

Silently, my eyes scanned the perimeter of the barn and all along the tree line.

Had I imagined he was with her the other night? *No, no way. I know what I saw. I saw her face, if just for a second... A secret nighttime meeting, but what was it for?*

I couldn't help feeling a flush of disappointment. No sightings with the woman meant no evidence to show Aunt Sara. Inevitably, that meant no potential blackmail leverage for me...

I was relieved to learn he wasn't doing anything worse, either—drug deals in the dark, or something of a scandalous danger that would pose a threat to my daughter.

I was gripping my phone so tightly my knuckles ached. And speaking of aches, my knees were killing me. I moved from my knees onto my haunches, shuffling a centimeter at a time to avoid any crackling in the brush underfoot.

Just as I was settling into a better position, the door to the shed peeked open. My uncle slid through a narrow gap in the doors, looked around, eyes passing right over where I was crouched, and then he used a thick metal padlock to lock the doors.

What is he hiding in there? My mind spun its own wild hypothesis: *perhaps my uncle is selling drugs and the woman he meets up with late at night is his drug dealer.*

It was ridiculous, of course. I'd never even seen Francis consume a glass of wine, much less something illegal and deadly like drugs. But it was strange... And he'd seemed concerned about making too much noise as he scanned his surroundings in the dark. The most likely conclusion was that he needed to lock up because there were expensive tools inside the shed, but I couldn't shake the feeling that something was off. *Why did he come out here so late at night? What is he hiding?* I wondered, once again.

As my uncle moved closer to my hiding spot, my stomach fluttered with fear. The nighttime bugs and amphibians were inconveniently silent now as I tried not to breathe.

But then I heard the crunch of gravel as he turned, followed by the snapping of twigs. My uncle was to the left of me, moving down the path he'd originally followed, headed back toward the house.

I closed my eyes, silently praying that he hadn't seen or heard me on his way back through.

The last thing I wanted to do was move from my hiding spot, but I needed to see where he was going next. Silently, I moved through the forest, ducking behind trees, moving stealthily beside him, incognito, as he followed the path back home.

Moonlight cut like a golden blade, and for brief flickers of time, I could see his dark eyes and ruddy downturned expression as he strolled along the path.

I stood there, lingering at the edge of the forest as he crossed the garden and returned to the house. Minutes passed, but they might as well have been hours. The gargoyles were watching me, their gunmetal-gray eyes a warning from above.

My uncle had gone inside; there was nothing keeping me from returning to the shed to explore. But my heart was still pounding—how would I explain my presence out here if he came back and found me? Or if he caught me slipping in the house behind him? What would my excuse be, for following him like a ghoul through the shadows and trees…?

He's not coming back. You have to move. You have to.

The silence was quieter this time around, as I followed the windy path back toward the shed. It seemed darker, too. I was tempted to take out my useless cell phone and utilize the torch option to guide me, but I couldn't take the chance of Francis or Sara peering through the windows, spotting the firefly light of my torch moving through the trees.

One foot in front of the other, my body shook with relief as the gap in the trees appeared once again. Silently, I crept through the knee-high grass and approached the ugly decrepit building my uncle had gone in earlier. Shivering, I wished I'd worn more than my holey Radiohead T-shirt. It was the end of summer, but it felt like mid-fall with the icy brush of wind on my shoulders.

Just as my uncle had earlier, I looked left and right, making sure the coast was clear before approaching the double doors of the shed. As I knew they would be, the doors were locked, secured by a medium-sized padlock. I tugged on it, half-heartedly.

My mind was spinning, thoughts tangling wildly. I imagined a secret lover's lair behind these doors—a creepy S&M room for rendezvous with his mistress. *Shouldn't have read all those* Fifty Shades of Grey *books*, I thought, frowning at the mystery.

I'd never seen Uncle Francis working on projects or coming out to use the building before now. I moved around the side of the shed, located two windows on either side. Both were foggy with dirt and grime, impossible to see inside. And most importantly: all locked up tight.

I'd failed at catching my uncle doing something unsavory, and I'd failed to get inside the shed. But I wouldn't give up that easily.

Tomorrow was Sara's second day to volunteer at the school and as usual, Francis and Gemma had work and school.

I know how to break inside an outbuilding, unfortunately. Finn and I, toward the end of his life, had been desperate for money. We'd used a hammer once, and bolt cutters twice, to get inside our neighbor's outbuildings. Remembering those days brought back a sick rush of guilt and shame. *I can't believe that was me, stealing a few tools and gadgets from others to pawn for money for drugs. How could that person… that person who stole and lied and snuck around… how could that same person be me?*

Tomorrow I planned to do it again. Perhaps my decision was just as shady as before, but this time it felt more noble. *I know Francis is hiding something, and I need to know what it is.*

Chapter Sixteen

STEP 7: HUMILITY

In the morning, I forced down breakfast, the taste like dirt in my mouth.

Sara was quiet, picking at her eggs and grits. I refused to break the awkward silence myself. Finally, she spoke: "I'm volunteering again today. I'll be gone until three. Do you mind thawing out the lamb? Maybe chopping some vegetables for supper?"

My eyes rose from my plate. Sara's voice was pleading. As I looked at her face, I caught a glimpse of something I hadn't seen before: worry. *Is she having more bouts of confusion?*

"Sure. Of course. Is there anything else you need done today?" I asked. In reality, I had plenty of plans of my own —rummaging through Francis's things and breaking into his secret shed. Snooping around, looking for proof of his indiscretions—whatever those might be.

But I couldn't lose this moment—a rare moment to help

out Aunt Sara. *I need her on my side when we go back to court. I need her to stop being Francis's puppet.*

"There's a bit of laundry in the dryer in the basement. I completely forgot about it. You could fold that, too, if you'd like. And the windows could really use a good scrubbing, but that's a big job. We could work on that together this weekend, perhaps?" She smiled warmly at me.

Surprised by her sudden change in demeanor, all I could do was nod. Once again, she was acting differently without Francis around. Was it possible she was scared of him? And, if so, then why? What was he doing to her to make her so afraid? Her strange changes in behavior solidified my suspicions of Francis. *If she's afraid of him, then maybe Gemma is too.*

My mind fluttered with a million thoughts. I tried not to imagine him—*right now, at this very moment*—driving my daughter to school.

"And if you need to do some laundry of your own, there's detergent and everything else you need down in the basement, on a shelf near the washer and dryer," Sara said.

"Okay. Thank you. I'll wash up these plates too, so you can get to work," I offered, pushing back my chair. Truth was, I was eager—butterflies zipping around in my stomach as I thought about my plans for snooping.

Sara passed her half-full plate to me and I stacked it on top of mine. "Thank you, Norah. Listen, I know it might not seem like it, but I'm glad you're here. In many ways, you remind me of your mother."

Those words stopped me in my tracks. This was the first time she'd mentioned my mother.

"Oh, really? What reminds you of her?"

Sara shook her head and laughed, pushing back her chair as she stood. She gripped the back of her chair with both hands. For the first time, I noticed how old and fragile she was.

"It's nothing really. Hard to pinpoint. Maybe it's your voice or your smile, or a little bit of both, I think... And you look so much like her." I imagined my mother when I was younger, bent down before me, smile stretching so wide it reached her eyes. Her hair was thick and dark like mine, and we both had the same eyes. But nothing about us was the same; she was thin, and I had always been chubby. Her long legs dwarfed my stubby five-foot frame. And she was always responsible, conservative, keeping her emotions close to the vest.

"I miss her," I said.

Sara shook her head, sadly. "Me too, Norah. Me too."

I set to work with paper towels and window cleaner, scrubbing at the grimy old pane in the kitchen.

A few moments later, Sara was at the front door, heavy purse draped over her forearm. "Call me if you need anything, okay?" I almost mentioned my phone getting disconnected but decided not to. I had no reason to call her back home. In fact, I needed her to stay gone as long as possible today.

"I will," I said.

"See you later," Sara chirped, poking her head in the

kitchen. She had pinned her long hair into a loose chignon at the nape of her neck.

"See you then." I moved to the front window. Humming, I cleaned in slow circles as I watched her Taurus back down the long, twisty driveway, then slowly disappear. *I hope Merrill doesn't show up again, secretly checking up on me and taking the opportunity to scold me.* I rolled my eyes at the memory.

Chapter Seventeen

The basement was cobwebby and dark—just as I'd imagined it would be.

I had so few things to wash—so few things I *owned*—but I dumped my leggings from last night, as well as a few T-shirts and panties, in the wash and, after figuring out how the buttons worked on the ancient machine, set it on a quick spin cycle.

The last thing I wanted to do was waste time, but I forced myself to wait a few more minutes... just in case Sara had forgotten something and turned back around. The last thing I needed was her or, worse, Francis, catching me snooping. With my past, they would undoubtedly assume the worst—that I planned on stealing from them. But as much as they didn't trust me, the feeling was mutual.

As the washing machine whipped and whirled noisily, I folded Sara's laundry from the dryer then inspected the rest of the basement.

Despite the earthy dirt floors and concrete, the space was fairly neat. Christmas decorations in one corner. A few sacks of old clothes in tubs labeled "For Goodwill" in the other. Next to the Christmas décor was a hodge-podge of items, including two framed photographs of Sara and Francis. In each they were younger, the photos black and white. They were happy, smiling, as they stood shoulder to shoulder. In the second photo, however, Francis's face was turned. Staring at his beautiful bride with what could only be construed as admiration.

Using my thumb, I wiped the dust from his face. *It's almost like he adores her here.* Even with his height and broad shoulders, he looked small beside her in this photo.

What happened between them? Now she seems like the one catering to his every whim.

Carefully, I set the photos aside. What interested me most was the long metal work bench in the corner and the massive peg board on the wall behind it, displaying a plethora of tools. *This is exactly what I need to get in that shed.*

Neat rows of screwdrivers and wrenches were laid across the bench. Unlike the rest of the basement, these weren't coated in dust. *Maybe Uncle Francis was outside working on a project last night. And the woman could have been a family member or friend.* I groaned.

My eyes drifted to the peg board. Machete. Scythe. Axe. Hammer. The machete and the axe gave me pause. I knew some people were collectors of tools, but seeing the sharp blades unnerved me. *What does Uncle Francis need a machete for? To keep Aunt Sara in line?* I thought, grimly.

What I really needed was a pair of bolt cutters, and there were none to be seen.

Finally, I reached up and took down the hammer. The lock wasn't tiny, but it wasn't the biggest I'd seen either. A few good knocks with the hammer and I'd have it off there in no time.

The thought of taking out Francis's lock was terrifying. There was no way he wouldn't notice it. But at least I'd have plausible deniability. A broken lock might be proof of a crime, but there was no way to prove I'd done the deed. *Hopefully…*

I carried the hammer upstairs, checking one more time through the front window to make sure the coast was clear.

Moments later, I was outside—the sun bright and warm on my skin as I made my way down the beaten path in the woods. The trees were beautiful, the forest full of life at this time of day… *Much better than being out here at night.*

I shimmied down the pathway, holding the hammer close to my side, until I emerged at the rickety old shed once again. In the light of day, it looked decrepit. Shingles clung to the rooftop, the few windows grimy and cracked. There were vines, long and reaching, like alien tentacles, that were bound to consume the building itself.

Briefly, I considered what would happen if I used the hammer on a window instead. *Hell, there's already spidery cracks in a couple of them anyway…*

But the windows were high, and I wasn't sure if I'd have the strength to reach them, much less pull my entire body through the glassy holes I'd make.

I approached the locked doors, gripping the hammer tightly. No one was around; I was basically in the middle of no-fucking-where, in a field shielded by ancient old trees on both sides... but I couldn't shake this feeling. *A feeling I was being watched.*

I scanned the tree line, for animal or man, but found nothing.

Taking a deep breath, I swung the hammer with all my might. The lock fell to my feet on the first try.

"Well, there's no going back now." I snatched up the lock, tucking it inside my jean pocket. I'd figure out what to do with it later. *Perhaps leave it on the ground or toss it deep in the woods?* I considered my options.

When I flung the doors open, I was hit by a musty, thick wall of dust. It brought back a memory—not one of those drug-related flashbacks, but something else. Something long and nearly forgotten from my childhood... my mother's shed, dusty and dank, filled with old hardcover books, their covers so worn I couldn't read the titles. I'd created stories with them—magic books filled with ancient spells...

Once again, my mind returned to the closed-off hallway and eerie room upstairs. And the picture of a little girl... *Constance, age five.*

Who was she?

Shaking off the thoughts, I stepped inside the shed and pulled the heavy doors closed behind me.

As I surveyed the tiny space, which was basically more like an abandoned shack, my addict brain immediately clocked the bottles that were lined on a low-leaning shelf. A pint of vodka, half empty. Or half full if you're so inclined. And more—three shot-sized bottles of Jack Daniel's and a fifth of Everclear—190-proof grain alcohol. The mere sight of the bottle sent shivers from my scalp all the way down my spine. It was popular in America; not unusual to find it here, but the memories it triggered made my stomach fill with knots.

When they say pick your poison... I can honestly say that alcohol was never mine.

AA wasn't just for alcoholics. The program was supposed to work for a variety of addictions, and many of the people I'd met along the way suffered from all kinds.

I drank very little as a teen, and my late teen years and early twenties were swept away when I became pregnant with Gemma. I preferred the smooth-sailing relief that only came from doing opioids. But when Finn and I couldn't get those, we supplemented however we could. The uppers were the worst; amphetamine led to insomnia and, eventually, drug-induced psychosis at times. But it was the alcohol, mixed with the opioids, that killed him on that fateful night.

The bottle of Everclear was lying on its side in the kitchen. It was half full when I left for work that day. It was empty when I came home. Along with our entire leftover stash of Oxy from the weekend. Mixing the two together was what essentially led to Finn's death. He lost consciousness, his heart rate and breathing slowing until they stopped forever. I could see it so clearly in my mind—

there's me, curled up like a cat beside him, waiting for the paramedics to arrive...

Finn is gone forever. Someday, I'll probably forget the exact details of his face... but no time soon.

My hands shaking, I reached for the bottle of Everclear on the shelf.

It's not the same. Not the same bottle. And drinking it won't bring Finn back either.

But drinking will do one thing—it'll push me further away from my daughter, set me spiraling out of control once more. No, I won't do it. I've come too far.

For a moment I was hit with the strangest sensation— that my hands were moving without my consent, twisting at the top... that I couldn't stop myself from drinking.

I could drink it. I could drink all of it. Everything in here. I could forget, however briefly, what it feels like to lose the man I love. To lose my sweet daughter... They're never going to give her back, so fuck it! Why not forget everything for a moment? One sip would feel like nothing. A few sips would take the edge off. It's not like I'd drink the entire thing. Not like Finn. Not like Finn...

I slammed the bottle back on the shelf and turned away, swallowing my pain. *Living sober takes a lot more guts than living high.* I don't remember who said those words, but it was someone in my AA group at the rehab center. Those words clawed at my brain, sunk their talons into my heart permanently. *Want to be brave?* I could hear her voice, see the web of crow's feet engraved around her lips. *Want to be a daredevil? Then try walking through this world every single day stone-cold sober, remembering your mistakes and spending every moment of your life making up for them. I dare you.* Her words like a mantra in my gullet, I turned my back on the booze.

I will make it up to Gemma. I have to. It's my fault she's here and we're in this mess to begin with.

I scanned the rest of the contents in the barn. More tools out here. Chainsaw. Pickax. A bundle of rope. Two plastic canisters of gasoline. Some old barrels.

Basically, it's what you'd expect to find in a dilapidated shed in the forest behind a gothic old house.

But that didn't explain my uncle's clandestine trip out here at night under the cover of darkness... and I couldn't see any projects...

Yes, there is an explanation, I realized. *There is an addict living in his house. A woman he can't trust.* And I hadn't seen an ounce of alcohol inside the house, not in the cupboards or refrigerator. Although I'd like to say that I didn't check, there's always a part of me that's searching, clocking all my options. There were none inside my uncle and aunt's home. *Because all the booze is hidden out here,* I realized.

Francis probably snuck out here for a quick nightcap. God, how stupid can I be! He came out here to get drunk, far away from me! And now I'm standing here with his broken lock in my pocket, surrounded by the booze he hid from me! If that doesn't make me look guilty, I don't know what does...

Now I'd gone and really screwed up. Breaking into the shed... *stupid stupid stupid. He'll know it was me, obviously. He'll assume I was imbibing his booze stash. He'll probably tell the judge when we return to court... fuck fuck fuck.*

I whipped around on my heels, ready to make a run to

the hardware store. *There has to be something I can do to fix this, and fast! I need someone to fix this lock... I need to put it back exactly as it was...*

Running for the doors, panic exploding in my veins, my foot struck the side of an old steel barrel. I drew in a sharp breath through my teeth, toe surging with pain.

I limped back over to the drum and gave it a once-over. It was old, orange with rust. Faded letters on the side of it. God knew how long it had been out here.

Perhaps it was sheer desperation, the hope that I'd find something, *anything* to give me leverage over Francis, that made me want to open the barrel.

In my darkest fantasies, I imagined throwing the lid off of it and discovering kilos of illegal drugs. *Maybe Francis is a drug dealer. Or maybe he's making his own drugs, Walter White-style.*

So, that's why I unloosened the bolt. That's why I removed the ring that was holding the lid in place. That's why I lifted the lid of the barrel...

And that's how I found the body.

Chapter Eighteen

When I was in college, I took an art class. The dumbest decision I ever made. Not because the class wasn't a good one—it was. But because I'd made the silly mistake of assuming it would be easy. An uncomplicated elective; a break from math, science, and English.

But as it turns out, introductory art design and appreciation is hard as hell when you have no experience, or interest, in *making* art. The first task I was assigned was to draw a bowl full of apples. Again and again, I tried to make that stupid bowl, until finally, I went to my art professor and requested to drop her class. She said no. Instead, she sat down with me and taught me to look between the lines.

I wasn't drawing the bowl of fruit in front of me on the table. Instead, I was drawing one piece at a time—a line here, a curve there, a shadow underneath...

She taught me to see the whole in parts—to pick it apart and work it slowly, step by step.

Perhaps that's why I can't see the big picture now.

I see the curve of a shoulder.

The ashy point of an elbow.

Wiry bits of string attached to a soggy black circle… *hair.*

And a dome of rotted, black fruit… but beneath the dome is a moon-white face.

Bloated blue lips and owlish eyes… the neck bent so that the face is looking straight up at me.

Oh, sweet Jesus, what have I found…

The lid clattered to the dirt floor with a bang, and I scurried backward like a crab to escape the dead woman in the barrel. Vomit came before I could stop it, oozing down my chin, and then as I fell forward on my knees, it splashed on the floor in front of me.

Now that the lid was off, I could smell her. *There's no mistaking that smell.* It's the smell of decomposition. A smell I know… but not like this. *I've never smelled anything like this. Oh God…*

Moments later, I was back on my feet, sliding around the floor in my own spew as I bolted back outside.

I'm screaming. I could hear myself doing it, but it didn't sound right, the screech of madness so unlike me. And the sound of it so loud, so guttural, it had to echo for miles.

I ran for the first thing I could see… *the truck.*

Door locked.

Oh my God. Oh my God. Oh my God. I have to get out of here! I have to call the police! I have to get my daughter. Away from this man, this family… away from this fucking hideous place!

I tried the passenger side door of the truck. Also locked.

"Shit!" I screamed, slamming my palm against the truck window.

Left with no other choice, I took off running through the woods.

Keys. I know where they are… Think, Norah, think!

I saw a few loose keys in a kitchen drawer, just yesterday. Could one of those possibly belong to the truck?

With my phone disconnected and no landline, I had no way to call for help… Perhaps I could run to the nearest neighbors, but that would take so long… too many miles!

That crazed maniac is going to pick up my daughter from school; I have to get to her first!

I was halfway down the footpath leading back to the house when I realized my own stupid mistake. I stopped, panting and bent over, then I removed my phone from my pocket.

My phone was disconnected, sure. But it wasn't entirely useless. You could still call 911 from defunct cell phones. I didn't know where I'd heard that, but I prayed it was true as I punched in the code for the lock screen and dialed 911.

"Oh, thank God," I gasped, as a female dispatcher came on the line. "I'd like to report a body. I found a body in my uncle's shed…"

Chapter Nineteen

I didn't wait for the cops to arrive.

In the kitchen, I found just what I needed—a silver ring with two identical Ford keys. These must belong to the truck.

I knew I should wait for the cops, but I'd told the dispatcher everything I knew on the phone. The last thing I wanted was to stick around and wait for Francis or Sara to show up... Most importantly, I had to get my daughter immediately.

Francis was insane; that much was clear. I couldn't let him catch wind of the cop's discovery and try to kidnap my daughter from school.

Heart pounding like a steady drum, I took the keys and returned to the shed. I tried not to look through the open shed doors to the hideous barrel inside them, and what I knew it contained. *Who is she? Why is he keeping her here? Just how crazy is my uncle?*

And where the hell are the cops? I wondered, unlocking the truck door and jumping into the cab. Beads of sweat rolled down the back of my T-shirt as I stuck the key in the ignition. *Please work.*

The old truck fired up on the first try.

"Thank fucking God," I muttered under my breath. I shifted the truck into gear and went barreling through the field. I drove for miles until I reached civilization, finally connecting with an old dirt road. I prayed it would lead me to Restoration.

The only thing that matters now is protecting Gemma.

Chapter Twenty

I didn't bother with parking. Slamming on the parking brake, I left the truck at the curb in front of Restoration.

"I don't give a shit what they have to say this time. I'm taking my daughter," I hissed through clenched teeth as I jerked on the first set of double glass doors.

My body was a live wire, adrenaline soaring, thoughts whirling out of control. *There's a dead fucking body in my uncle's shed. The same uncle my daughter has been living with for three fucking months. How could I let these people keep my daughter?*

But I'd deal with that later—my mind was on a one-way track: *GET GEMMA.*

Through another set of double doors, I ran into my first roadblock. The doors I'd breezed through on my first visit were locked up tight during school hours.

I banged my fists on the glass, looking for signs of life

through the glass. The hallways were empty, not a teacher or aide in site.

I kept banging, for what felt like several minutes, before I saw the bell on the wall. *Please ring the bell and wait for an office member to greet you. Please have your ID ready*, it read.

I didn't have my ID. I didn't have anything on me besides the clothes on my back and the keys to the old Ford wedged in my fist.

Finger pressed to the bell, I kept ringing and ringing until a familiar face appeared at the door. Principal Fulkerson, eyes wide with confusion, parted the door open a crack.

"I need Gemma now," I said, pushing my way inside.

"Excuse me! What do you think you're doing?" Mrs. Fulkerson shouted, but I was already on my way, headed down the first hallway to… *I don't know where Gemma's classroom is. I don't even know her teacher's name*, I realized. *Because I'm a shitty fucking parent and I let my daughter live with a fucking killer for three months.*

"Hey!" Mrs. Fulkerson grabbed on to the fleshy underside of my arm. "What the hell is going on?" she demanded.

"You can call the cops if you don't believe me. They're at the house now, Francis and Sara's…" I realized that my voice was too fast, my thoughts sped up so my words couldn't stay in tandem. *I missed my medicine this morning*, I thought. A strange time to remember now.

I took a deep breath, placing a hand on my chest to steady the rock-pounding dread in my chest.

"I found a body at my aunt and uncle's home. In their shed."

Principal Fulkerson's eyebrows shot up. "Excuse me. Did you say a body?"

There was motion in the hall behind me, other teachers and personnel coming out of their classrooms to see what the commotion was all about.

I lowered my voice, still trying to steady my breath. "There was a body of a woman in the shed at my aunt and uncle's home," I repeated, trying to remain as calm and quiet as possible. "Francis stuffed her inside a barrel like old trash."

The principal's face was sheet-white now. *At least she's taking me seriously.*

"Norah?" I felt a hand on my lower back, and then Jana was by my side. "Why don't we all go to my office and chat?" She was tugging on the back of my shirt now with a warning pull, leading me away from the crowd of gawkers.

Looking around at all the unfamiliar faces, shiny teachers and shiny students. Fresh faces filled with fear and confusion. Luckily, I didn't see Gemma. I didn't want her to find out the truth like this...

"Come on. Let's go," Jana urged, and I had no other choice but to follow. *At least they won't let Francis take my daughter anywhere, not until they have heard the full story and checked it all out with the police.*

I fell in step beside Principal Fulkerson and Jana, evading the eyes of teachers and aides with leery expressions. I could hear a few of them urging students back into their classrooms.

"I need someone to go fetch Gemma from her classroom now. She's not safe, not with that maniac Francis scheduled to pick her up today," I said, breathily.

"Don't worry. I'll send someone to check on Gemma now," Principal Fulkerson said. Her face had softened into worried lines, no longer the angry woman I'd met the other day. I watched as she turned her back to me and spoke quietly into her walkie talkie.

"In here," Jana said.

The three of us shuffled into a small office, not much bigger than a broom closet. Principal Fulkerson shut the door tightly behind us.

"Take a seat. And take a breath, Norah." Jana motioned at one of two chairs in front of her desk. I collapsed into one of them, breathing for the first time. I could barely remember the drive here...

Principal Fulkerson stayed by the door as Jana slipped behind the stiff metal desk.

"Start from the beginning, Norah. Tell us exactly what happened," Jana urged, giving me her full attention.

Chapter Twenty-One

The moment I got to the part of the story where I wrestled the lid off the barrel, Principal Fulkerson excused herself. *She's probably sick to her stomach, hearing this,* I thought.

"After I called the police, I took the keys to the truck and drove straight here. I know I should have stayed there and waited to speak with them, but I couldn't risk letting Francis pick up Gemma..."

I tried to catch Jana's eye, to assess her thoughts, but she was giving nothing away.

"Please. I need Gemma..." I needed her to do something. *Say something.* Give me some sort of reassurance...

"It'll be okay. We will figure this out. Just wait..." Jana said.

Suddenly, the door to the office swung open. I jumped in my seat, my own jerky movement startling Jana.

"It's just me," Principal Fulkerson said, frowning. She pulled the door partially closed behind her.

"Jana, could you excuse me and Mrs. Campbell, please?" Her voice was calm, *too calm*. I looked back and forth between them.

"Yes, absolutely." I watched Jana go. As she shuffled back out the office door, I saw two people standing out in the hallway. Policemen.

I pushed my chair back and stood.

"Stay calm, Norah. These officers just want to talk to you," Principal Fulkerson spoke softly, as though she were coddling a newborn baby.

"Did they arrest him yet? Did they see the body?"

I pushed past Mrs. Fulkerson and rushed out to see them before she could stop me. "Officers! Hello. I'm the one who called you. I found the barrel in my uncle's shed…"

There were two police officers standing with Jana in the hall, one of them so young he barely looked old enough to purchase cigarettes; the other, silver-headed and rough around the edges, looked like a less handsome, less badass version of Clint Eastwood.

"Miss." The young officer stepped in front of me, lifting his hands like a cross guard. And then he was reaching for me, hands touching my shoulders.

"Please don't touch me," I said, moving around him to speak to the older, more seasoned-looking officer.

"Did you get my daughter out of class? She needs to be with me. I need to know she's safe…"

When he looked at me with those hard, unfriendly eyes,

I shot a questioning look at Jana. Her lips were pursed, her eyes pupilless—*what is going on?* I wondered.

"If you all won't fetch Gemma for me, I'll get her myself!" As I tried to push by them, the older officer grabbed me forcefully by the wrist.

"You need to calm down, lady. You're not going into any classroom, and you don't even have legal custody of your daughter," he said.

"Excuse me?" I screamed. I tried to pull away from him, but his grip on my wrist only tightened. I could feel the younger officer behind me now too, breathing down my neck.

"Do you want me to put the cuffs on?" he squeaked, talking to the older officer.

"What? Why?" I tried again, unsuccessfully, to free myself.

"Hey, it's okay. That won't be necessary. Let's all go in the office and talk," Jana shushed me. She took my other arm, stroking it up and down, giving me a stone-cold look. *A warning look.*

Calm the fuck down, her eyes were saying.

"Yes, please. I want to know what's going on. I called you all for help. I haven't done anything wrong," I breathed.

As the officer released me and Jana coaxed me back inside the office, I realized a small crowd had gathered. I wouldn't swear to it, but I thought I saw Gemma on the outskirts, hands covering her face as she watched me go.

Chapter Twenty-Two

"I don't understand." I was slipping away, thoughts wandering through the depressing bricked-in halls of Restoration... and my body, I could feel it dissociating from my brain. *This can't be real this can't be real this can't be real...*

The older officer, Officer Dowdy, cleared his throat. Then he repeated himself. "There's no dead body in your uncle's shed. You must have made a mistake, or..."

"Or what?"

Officer Dowdy picked at his fingernails, as though he were bored. *Is a crazy killer who stuffed a body in a barrel not enough to pique his interest?*

"They found overturned alcohol bottles in the shed and vomit. Your uncle tells me you were just released from rehab." His eyes rose to meet mine; they were grey and steely in the gloomy, low-lit office.

"I wasn't drinking. I've been clean for nearly one hundred days... You can breathalyze me if you want."

"There's more."

"More? I don't understand!"

I could feel Jana's hand again, resting on the top of my leg. Trying to soothe me. *Or possibly trying to warn me...*

"Get the hell off me," I shoved her hand away. And when I did, I heard that bitch Fulkerson tsk tsk from her seat in the corner.

"There was a hypodermic needle in your suitcase, sewn into the nylon."

The room was spinning on its axis now, not enough air in the room to go around...

"But. But... wait. I completely forgot it was in there. It's been in my suitcase since before I left for rehab. You can check the needle! I haven't used it recently... and besides, what does this have to do with the body?"

"Like I said, we found no body," Officer Dowdy repeated, his voice growing louder and more impatient.

"It's inside the barrel... I left the lid off. I saw her face... I swear she's there... and that smell..." The odor didn't even fully register at first, I was in such shock when it happened. But now I could recall the smell, bring it back in my mind: a mixture of sweet rotting fruit and meat.

My stomach curled in on itself and I took a big breath, met with only stuffy, recycled air.

I need to get out of here. Out of this room! I stood up, slowly. The urge to run was insistent. Overpowering.

Get me away from here; I need to get my daughter and process what's happened...

"There *was* a barrel in the shed, ma'am." This voice came

from the young officer. Arms crossed over his chest, he kept picking at a scab on his elbow. I shot him a grateful look. *So, they did find the barrel. But…?*

"It was alcohol in the barrel. And yeah, it did smell. There were nasty chunks of fruit, corn maize, and barley in it, ma'am…"

"No. You're lying." That rotten smell… *No way it was alcohol. I saw a* face, *her shoulders… those stringy bits of what must have been hair…*

"Maybe it was the wrong barrel," I pleaded. "Or maybe he moved it!" I said, the thought just now occurring to me. I mean, he would have had to do it fast, but it was certainly possible… I remembered the overwhelming sensation I'd had right before I entered the shed—the feeling of being watched.

"We found no other barrels, outside or in. And Francis and Clara weren't home when we got there. No one was. In fact, Francis is working at the cement plant right now. We sent one of our officers over there to collect him. We're going to ask him some questions, but we've already spoken to him some. And we just talked to Sara, too. Your uncle's not supposed to be making his own moonshine, and he knows that. But that's a far cry from what you're claiming—a dead body in a barrel. So ridiculous," Officer Dowdy said, rolling his eyes at his partner.

"I don't understand…"

"The other thing they found." The young officer cleared his throat again, refusing to meet my eye.

"Oh, that's right. We found something else in your bedroom. A suicide note in your suitcase."

Jana let out a small gasp when he said it.

I winced.

"I can explain that, too," I said, the urge to vomit for the second time today growing by the minute. "I'm not suicidal. Not at all. That note was old…"

"There's no date on it. And we saw all your medications…"

"It's not a crime to be suicidal, or to take mental health meds," said Jana, her voice rising to defend me. *About time,* I thought, giving her a look that was a mixture of gratitude and surprise.

"No, it's not. But seeing as one side effect of SSRIs is hallucinations, we started to wonder… well, we're wondering if maybe you need some help, ma'am. Whether it's a mental break or you're back on the junk, we are here to assist you. Your aunt and uncle are petitioning for an emergency hold, to have you evaluated…"

"No!" I roared. My feet were moving now, rushing for the door. *How can this be real? I need to get my daughter and get the fuck out of this town. This town, with its rotting girls in barrels, crazy aunts and uncles, and shit-for-brain cops…*

I would go to every classroom if I had to, shouting my daughter's name. *We are getting away from here, court orders be damned! I grew her in my belly; I raised her from birth. Not a single soul in this world can stop me now! Gemma belongs to me!*

I was power walking down the hallway, arms chugging determinedly, when they took me down from behind.

Chapter Twenty-Three

STEP 8: WILLINGNESS

Three days later

The last person I expected to find waiting for me in the lobby was Jana.

She stood, slowly, clutching a large saddle bag to her waist. "I offered to come. Francis and Sara said it was okay," she explained, softly.

I nodded but said nothing. As Steve, the friendly orderly I'd grown accustomed to over the last couple days, led me to the front counter, Jana followed closely behind.

The receptionist sat behind the counter, shielded by a thick wall of plex-glass. "I've marked all of the spots you need to sign," she said, without a glance. She flipped through a thick stack of papers, pointing at little Post-its that were marked for my signature, with her long purple nails.

Wash, rinse, repeat.

"Thanks," I said, flatly, scratching my loopy signature in the blanks, not reading a bit of my discharge papers. I slid the stack back toward her and turned to Jana.

She nodded for me to follow her out.

I was quiet as I climbed in the passenger seat of her Plymouth, not trusting myself to speak.

"How are you?" Jana asked, tugging the seatbelt over her lap. I did the same, getting it caught in my hair.

I wasn't worried about me. That was the last thing on my mind. "How is Gemma? That's all that matters."

Jana started up the car. "She's doing fine, Norah. I saw her just before I came here. She was helping your Aunt Sara bake a pie for you. She said that rhubarb is your favorite…"

The thought of my daughter in *that* house…

And me, unable to do anything about it, made me feel so helpless… *worse* than helpless. I'd felt worthless these past few days, locked away in the behavioral health unit on a seventy-two-hour hold, judge's orders. *Courtesy of good old Uncle Francis.*

The ride was silent for several minutes. Then Jana turned on an unfamiliar road.

"Where are we going?"

"My place. It's only a few minutes from here," Jana said.

"What? No. I want to be with Gemma."

"It's just for the night. I'm taking you back there tomorrow…"

I wanted to argue. But as I'd learned over the last

seventy-two hours or so, what I wanted mattered very little. I'd given up my right to matter when I stuck that fucking needle in my arm two years ago.

I glared out the window, jaw clenching, as I recalled the shocking punch—or what I thought was a punch at first—of Officer Dowdy's taser on the back of my neck. The pain I could handle, even the humiliation, but the thought of Gemma left behind with those people, me unable to help her even if I'd wanted to, was all too unreal.

"Why? What's the point of me staying with you for one night? Did Francis say why?"

Jana shook her head, gold hoops swinging and getting caught in her hair, as she flipped on her turn signal and veered toward a narrow dirt road I'd never seen before.

"It wasn't his idea. It was mine. I was hoping we could talk first. Regroup before you go back. Make a game plan..."

"You want to be my therapist now?" I teased, the words flowing out harsher than intended.

"Definitely not. But I'd also like to think that I'm the closest thing you have to a friend in this town. You never got the chance to attend that AA meeting with me. I want to make sure your head is on straight before you go back there with Gemma..."

"I wasn't drinking in the shed. I told everyone that! Why won't anyone listen?" I growled. "I've been clean since I entered rehab, no mess-ups..."

"I believe you," Jana said, breathlessly.

"You do? Do you really?" I felt tired, perhaps from being overmedicated on the behavioral health unit—they'd added an extra anti-depressant to my daily regimen, even though I told them I didn't need it—or just exhausted with having to defend myself every single day of my life.

"I do believe you. But all that matters is what the judge believes, Norah."

Before I could respond, Jana was parking in front of a cottage. It was a tiny building, constructed of wood and stone, flanked by two chimneys on either end. The porch was covered with hanging flowerpots. Window boxes sprouted a colorful assortment of flowers. It resembled a gingerbread house, small and whimsical, like something from the Brothers Grimm.

And you know how well that story turned out, I thought, sulkily, removing my seatbelt.

"This is me," Jana said, giving me a weary smile. I unlocked my door and climbed out, stretching my legs.

"Come on. I'll make us some cookies and tea," Jana offered. I shivered.

_____

The inside of Jana's cottage was quaint, but messier than I'd expected. There were paperback books stacked on every open surface, and a corkboard overflowing with flyers and notices in the kitchen. As I stood at the board, I flipped through pages—local notices for AA meetings, church events, community affairs…

"Here." Jana handed me a stout cup of Earl Grey, then motioned me into the adjacent living room. There was a cracked leather sofa and a couple of worn armchairs arranged around an old stone fireplace.

"I'd apologize for all the book clutter, but I'm not sorry." Jana smiled over her cup of tea, as I got settled on the sofa across from her. "I love to read," she explained, taking a slow sip.

"Me too."

Sitting here, across from her like this, made me feel like I was back in therapy. Friendship be damned. I barely knew this woman. *Who can I trust these days? Only my damn self. And Gemma. Maybe not even myself,* I considered.

"How was the hospital?" she asked, finally, after I refused to initiate.

I shrugged. "Fine. I didn't need to go. Francis just wanted me out of his way."

Jana set her cup down on an old, scarred end table and gave me a serious look.

"The judge pushed your court date back a couple more days, per Francis and Sara's request. They figured you needed more time before the hearing, or else the judge would have ruled for them to continue with temporary custody. Did they tell you?"

I nodded. "Sara called me a couple times while I was in there. She sounded sorry. Deep down, she has to know what Francis is involved in…" I wondered aloud.

"Involved in what exactly?"

I sighed. There was no reason to repeat the story. It was obvious that no one believed me.

As though she could read my mind, Jana said, "So, you weren't drinking or using anything at your aunt and uncle's house?"

I shook my head. Sipped my tea. *She can either believe me or not. At least I know the truth. I'm so tired of trying to convince everyone!*

"Tell me about the needle. Also, tell me about the note."

I groaned. "What, are you reporting to the court now or something? Why are you involved in this, Jana?"

She smiled, tightly. "Because I care, Norah. That's why. And because I want to help you. I just need you to be honest with me..."

Honesty. As much as I tried to give it, some days it felt like it didn't matter anymore.

"Okay," I sighed. "After Finn died, I never got to mourn him, you know? Instead of treating me like a grieving spouse, they treated me like a criminal. I guess, in their eyes, that's exactly what I was. The paramedics and the medical examiner were removing his... his body—" I choked on the words and stopped for another sip of tea. It was tasteless, and it burned all the way down to my gullet.

Finally, I continued: "The cops were also called in immediately. Because of the drugs and the blood... and... and..."

"And they took you away. Arrested you instead of helping you, or consoling you," Jana finished.

I nodded.

"But one of the cops was pretty nice. I could tell she felt bad for me. But there were drugs in our bedroom, paraphernalia in our bedroom drawers… and they didn't know if his death was accidental or not at first. Anyways, I don't wholly blame them. What were they to do?"

Jana was quiet, her expression unreadable. So, I continued.

"I spent two nights in jail, only to find out that I had to stay even longer when I was released. Probation violation from my previous offense. They turned around and locked me back up. I didn't get to go to Finn's funeral. Not that his family would have allowed it anyway."

"Then what?" Jana pressed.

"Then finally, two long months later, after rotting in that jail, they granted temporary custody of Gemma to my aunt and uncle, who showed up out of the blue, and they ordered me to go to rehab. I had less than a few hours to pack."

"So, why did you take the needle?"

"Oh, I'm sure you can guess. As soon as I got back there, to that hellish apartment, every memory I'd ever had, with Gemma and Finn, all came flooding back to me, the good and the bad. The downright ugly. And, although the cops had cleaned the place out pretty good for drugs, there were a couple needles left behind. When you're an addict, you get good at hiding things."

Jana nodded, knowingly.

"I had a needle but no heroin. If I'd had enough money, or found drugs there that day, well…"

"You probably would have used."

"I would have. I was desperate to stop the intrusive thoughts, the regrets about what I'd done to Gemma, how I lost Finn and then I lost her but in a different way... It all felt so surreal, even then. And yes, there was even a part of me that wanted to die that day. I know it's my fault Gemma is with them. I can't take back my mistakes, but I sure as hell can try to fix it now.

"So," I continued, "I took the needle with me, just in case. It felt better to have it on me. Like a dog with a bone, I needed to keep my crutch close by. And the letter—I wrote that too. Because I thought about it that day in the apartment. Not because I wanted to end my suffering, but because I wanted to end everyone else's. I felt like everyone would be better off. That without me, Gemma could go on, have a better life without me in it."

If Jana was surprised by all this, she didn't show it.

"When did all that change?"

"About thirty days into treatment. The meds they gave me started working. I was feeling the effects of the pills, the cloud of depression lifting, and the cravings were all but gone once I shook off the withdrawals. I was dealing with the grief, best as I could. My doctor and therapist were amazing."

"So, why keep the needle? And the suicide note? Why not throw them out?"

"To be honest, I forgot about the needle after a while. And the note... well, it served as a reminder. I never wanted to forget how low I'd been, what the drugs and the loss caused me. I never want to go back to who I was before, that woman who almost tied a noose around her neck the day before she left for rehab."

Jana smiled, tenderly. "You're brave as hell, Norah. Has anyone ever told you that?"

I thought about it. "I don't think so. And I don't feel brave. I feel like a fucking coward. A coward who can't even convince people I'm telling the truth, who can't even protect her own daughter." The tears were forming now, stinging my eyes. I shook my head, trying to fight them off.

"And, you want to know the funny part? None of this has a damn thing to do with what I found in my uncle's shed, but since I'm an addict... well, you know the rest."

"You know how to tell when an addict's lying, don't you?" Jana said, a tiny, upturned smile on her lips.

"Their lips are moving," I answered, dully. I'd heard that stupid joke so many times I couldn't count. It was funny—in an uncomfortable way—the first few times I heard it in rehab. Now it just sounded ignorant.

"It's a dumb joke," Jana said, reading my mind. "And it's blatantly false. Because active users are often dishonest, yes. We do whatever it takes to keep our addiction under wraps, but once we're clean, shouldn't we be absolved of that liar's chair? Just because we were liars once, doesn't mean we're liars forever..."

I couldn't help the tears this time. They flowed down my cheeks, stinging my chafed lips.

"Exactly. Everyone thinks I'm lying about what I found. So, what am I supposed to do about it, then?"

Jana frowned. "You can't control anyone else, Norah, only you."

"I know that. Better believe that I know that…"

"I talked to Sara. She had a look at your discharge papers from your stint in rehab."

My lips puckered from the tea, a flicker of heartburn forming. "I know. I gave them to her," I said, swiping at my cheeks.

"Yeah, that's what she told me. She was worried about some of the things mentioned in the history portion of your admission. The psychosis you experienced when you lived with Finn."

I rolled my eyes. "Yes, I had hallucinations, but that was only when I was high on drugs, Jana."

"What about the incident with the knife in your neighborhood? It mentions it briefly in the paperwork but doesn't go into much detail."

I could imagine how this conversation between Jana and Aunt Sara had gone. Reading into every line of the initial report, making a big deal out of nothing.

But it wasn't nothing. Not when it happened.

"When you can't do opioids, your body goes into withdrawal."

"I know," Jana said.

"So, when Finn and I tried to kick the heroin, we used other drugs to help ride out the withdrawals. Like methamphetamine, for instance."

"You were high on meth, walking around your

neighborhood with a knife?" Jana said, eyebrows raising so high, they disappeared below her fluffy bangs.

"I guess you could say that. I hadn't slept in days and I thought taking a walk would wear me out. But my brain was misfiring, as it often does on drugs... I was worried about rapists in the neighborhood. There was a report of a rape two towns over. My over-amplified brain thought carrying a knife at my side during my late-night stroll was okay. I didn't hurt anyone with the knife. But when I returned, the cops were waiting. A neighbor had spotted me through his window and called it in."

My stomach churned with embarrassment as I remembered the incident. Not only could I remember what happened, I could close my eyes and drift back to that moment, that amped-up fear and adrenaline, unable to shut my body or mind off for days. It had felt so real in that moment... the fear and the fierceness.

"That was the last time I used any other drugs besides my prized heroin," I said, bitterly.

"I can see why," Jana said. "Listen. I'm not trying to badger you, I'm really not. I'm just sort of preparing you for what's going to happen when you go back to court. Your aunt and uncle, the doctors... There are a lot of things working against you when it comes to taking Gemma back."

"Gemma is my daughter. I screwed up before, but I'm clean now..."

"Of course she is. But Francis is determined not to relinquish custody, at this point."

"Then why are they letting me come back? Why not just tell me to take a hike and 'We'll see you in court?'" I wondered aloud.

Jana shrugged. "Honestly, I don't know the answer to that. Maybe they truly care for you."

But I knew the real reason. *Francis is possessive. He'd rather keep his enemy close. In case he has to stuff his enemy into a barrel and hide them away in his shed.*

"It's crazy when you think about it," I said, releasing a strange, inappropriate chuckle that caught both of us by surprise.

"What is?" Jana asked.

"There's a man with a dead body in his shed and then there's me, the former junkie. Still, I'm the villain. Always the fucking villain…"

Jana got to her feet, pacing back and forth in front of the fireplace. I watched her, trying to decipher the look on her face.

Finally, she stopped moving and came over to sit beside me. "Are you absolutely sure you saw what you say you saw?"

I thought about the hallucinations and delusions I'd suffered when I was high on drugs. They had felt so real, but they weren't.

This was different though; I was clear-headed when I found the barrel. That rotten head, stringy bits of scalp and hair… *No, I couldn't have imagined that.*

"I know what I saw," I said.

"You're sure you didn't just smell something funky, or

lift the lid and see fruit, rotten and fleshy, in the barrel and freak out because of your PTSD over Finn?"

I held my hands together, as though in prayer, and lifted my hands to my face as those bloated lips and dead gray eyes came floating back into my memory. For a moment, it was Finn's face I saw, not the dead woman in the barrel.

"I wasn't drinking. I wasn't high. I'd seen Francis outside late at night, with another woman, the night before. I decided to take a look in the shed while my aunt and uncle were both gone... and that's when I made the mistake of lifting the lid on the barrel."

"But... why did you jump in the truck and leave? What the hell were you thinking?" Jana pushed me.

"I wasn't thinking! My brain was in full Gemma-mode. I called the cops before I left. To be honest, I didn't care about preserving the scene or the body, or making sure Francis and Sara were investigated—I didn't care about any of that at the time. All I cared about was reaching Gemma at the school, getting her as far away from that dangerous predator as possible. I never imagined it would get turned around on me like this. Or that someone would switch out the barrel before the cops got there."

Jana shook her head back and forth. Again, I wondered if she thought I was lying. Or worse, delusional.

"Look, I know it sounds crazy..."

"It does. And you do. But I sort of believe you. At least I want to. You know how I feel about Francis. He's rubbed me the wrong way ever since he enrolled Gemma at Restoration..."

"See? Great minds think alike," I said, grabbing her hand in mine. I don't know why I felt so excited… It was just such a relief to have someone considering my version of events, taking me seriously, even just a little bit.

"But why would he do it? And… who the hell was in that barrel?" Jana said, throwing up her hands.

"Well, I can't tell you why. There's no good reason for stuffing a woman in a barrel, no matter how she died," I said. "But what about local missing women? You would have a better idea of who she might be…"

Jana frowned. "Honestly, I don't know. We don't have anyone missing from around here."

"Bullshit," I said, a little louder than intended. "Women go missing every day in this country. And even small towns like this one aren't immune. People kill us, rape us, kidnap us… Sometimes they simply make us disappear. Listen, that woman is somebody's person. Someone in this town is missing their wife, their daughter, their friend! They have to be," I said, exasperated.

Jana was chewing on her thumbnail, eyes grainy with thought.

"You know someone, don't you?" I said, moving to the edge of my seat.

"Not really. It's just… the only thing that comes to mind is Patricia."

"She's gone missing?" I said, hopeful. I shrunk back, feeling awful at the level of excitement in my tone.

Jana shook her head. "No. Patricia is a friend of mine. She's been attending AA meetings at the church nearly as long as I've been alive. She has a granddaughter who ran away, I think. But that was a few years ago…"

I put my hands together, rocking back and forth with nervous anxiety. "Maybe she didn't run away, Jana. Maybe my shitbag uncle killed her," I said.

"**T**hanks for doing this," I said, for the third time, as Jana parked the bulky Plymouth at the curb in front of the pawnshop. There were no other cars in the lot, just a couple of vehicles parked at the side of the building, presumably belonging to employees.

"Is this really necessary?" Jana asked, pointing at the object in my hand.

I gripped the engagement ring, the princess-cut diamond jabbing my palm, as a painful reminder. I could still remember the day Finn bought it for me, grinning ear to ear as he watched me try on rings at the local jeweler in Irving Park. *It's too much*, I'd said, pointing at the 900-dollar price tag. For some people, a ring in that price range might seem minuscule, but for me... I'd never owned anything anywhere near that expensive, not clothes or jewelry or purses, not even furniture.

Please, just let me do this. I want this to be special. I've always dreamed of giving the woman I love a beautiful ring she can be proud of. And proud he was, that day. Finn had been working steady hours at his job as a cabinet maker, and he'd recently received a raise. This was before the drugs took over, before he shrunk before my eyes…

Every day up until the day he died, I wore that ring on my finger. Not only was it the most beautiful ring I'd ever seen, but every time I glanced at it, I was reminded of that bubbly feeling of joy that day at the jeweler's, and the giggly, awkward proposal that followed soon after.

I couldn't take it with me when I went to jail, or when I left for rehab. And since getting out, I'd worn it on a cheap chain around my neck. Wearing it on my finger would never be the same. Its luster was gone; without Finn, it no longer served its promised purpose.

Instead of reminding me of better times, the ring told a different story: a story of what might have been.

We could have been fucking great. We could have had it all.

"Yes, I'm sure," I said, turning back to Jana. "Finn, despite all his issues, loved Gemma dearly. He would want me to do whatever necessary to get back on my feet and take care of business."

"Okay." Jana shrugged, helplessly.

And that was that. I exited the car and walked inside the pawn shop, ready to part with the last thing I owned that connected me with my dead fiancé.

With six hundred dollars in my pocket, I asked Jana to drive me to Walgreen's next.

"I'll be just a minute." Twenty minutes later, I returned to the car with several bags slung over my arm.

"Anything good in there?" Jana asked, wiggling her eyebrows. I tried to imagine us on a normal day, hanging out as friends. How would it feel to have a normal girlfriend to hang out with? To run errands with? To trust with all my secrets?

As much as I wanted to get the hell out of this desolate town, I'd certainly miss Jana when I left it. She was tough, and asked too many questions, but she was real. And I needed more *real* in my life, these days.

"Depends on what you consider good," I teased, unloading the bags on the center console between us. I'd filled all of my prescriptions—the new medication, and refills for the ones that were due.

I'd also purchased a disposable cell phone, and a cache of at-home drug test kits.

"What are those for?" Jana pointed.

"If I'm going to get Gemma back, then I'm going to have to do more than just 'walk the line'. I'm going to have to have indisputable proof that I'm clean and capable of taking care of her."

Jana nodded along, smiling. "Damn right," she said.

"Will you watch me take a pee in these every day?" I asked, my face serious.

Jana chortled. "You want a witness, I guess?"

"Yes. Not only daily tests that show I'm clean, but someone to observe me taking them each day so that no one can say I tried to cheat them."

"For you, I'll do it," Jana said. "And the phone? What happened to your other one?"

"Disconnected." I ripped the plastic off the disposable phone and dug out the instructions on how to activate it. "My plan is to contact my former boss at the restaurant and get her to put it in writing that I have a job there. And then I'm going to have my landlord do the same. I need to be able to show the court that not only am I clean and stable, but I have a job and home to return to. I want Gemma to have a stable place to go, and I also need to show the judge that I'm capable of providing that."

"Very smart," Jana said. As I went to work activating the phone, she put the car in gear.

"And what about the body you found?" she said, voice barely above a whisper.

"I'm going to shut up about it for now. My best bet of getting my daughter back is to keep a low profile, please my aunt and uncle, and do everything by the book and document it up until my court hearing. It's important that I earn everyone's trust."

"Smart girl," Jana said, reaching over to squeeze my leg.

I tried not to flinch at her touch, focusing my eyes on the phone buttons in front of me.

It wasn't a lie. I did have to earn their trust, as well as Jana's. And she was wrong about what she said before, about addicts and lying. It wasn't when my mouth was moving that they needed to worry, it was when I went quiet.

And staying quiet is exactly what I plan to do.

Chapter Twenty-Five

J ana helped me unfold the bed from her pull-out couch in the den and showed me where the extra blankets were kept. Even though it had been a warm and sunny day, the wind was lashing through the trees outside, creating an icy breeze, and Jana decided to throw a few logs on the fire.

"It must be brilliant in the winter," I said, pointing at the fireplace as I tossed a white sheet over the bed and unfolded a dark green comforter.

"It is. I don't use the fireplace as often as I should."

I wanted to ask more about her life, the kind woman who'd taken me in for the night and befriended me, but who lived alone in this little gingerbread house on the edge of town.

"Are you sure the courts will approve of me staying here? I feel like I'm beholden to Francis and Sara these days."

Jana frowned. "They have temporary custody of Gemma, Norah. Not you. Plus, I discussed it with both Francis and Sara—"

Our conversation was interrupted by the dull dinging of the doorbell.

"Ah! There's the pizza," Jana said.

I tugged the comforter over the pull-out bed and followed her through the kitchen to the front door. She was paying a young pizza delivery boy, his face handsome but spotted with acne.

"Thanks, Joey. You're a lifesaver," she said, passing him a wad of bills with her free hand and balancing the big white pizza box in the other.

"I'm out of the delivery range out here, and Mama Jo's is the only decent pizza in town. I order so much pizza that they made an exception for me. And Joey never turns down a chance to deliver because I'm a great tipper," she smiled.

I took the box from her hands and carried it over to the small Formica table. It was a nice change from the ornate king's table at Francis and Sara's place.

"I take it you don't like to cook much."

Jana chuckled, taking a few plates and cups down from the cupboard. Her kitchen was tiny, with only a few cabinets on top and bottom, but I imagined she didn't need much storage for just one person.

"Actually, I enjoy cooking. I used to cook all the time when I was younger, for my siblings and my dad. But it takes the fun out of it when you're only cooking for one person. I do it a few nights a week. In fact, I made rigatoni and pot roast over the weekend because I was in the mood. But no matter how hard I try to plan out my portions, I always end up making too much food. Then I end up with a rotting roast in the fridge for weeks on end."

I swallowed a lump in my throat, thinking back to the rotting hunk of meat in Francis's shed. Those eyes, bottomless and bulgy staring back at me... The face waxy and surreal in the August heat. Where did he hide the barrel if it wasn't there when the police arrived?

"Here you go." Jana handed me a plate and I tried to shake off the memory. The pizza was thick, a fat layer of gooey cheese on top, thick bits of pepperoni and sausage hidden underneath.

"Hey, this a bit like what we have back home. Chicago style," I said, sliding two slices onto my plate and pulling up a chair next to Jana.

We were quiet for several minutes, both of us enjoying the fresh, hot slices, courtesy of Mama Jo herself.

"So, tell me more about you," I said, reaching for a paper towel with greasy fingers. I handed half of the towel to Jana and she wiped the grease from her lips.

"What do you want to know?"

"I don't know. Surprise me." I shrugged. I felt like I'd been a bad friend to Jana so far, talking so much about myself and my problems, dragging her into my family's drama.

"Well." Jana picked at her slice, thinking. "I like to write. It's one of the reasons I moved here."

"Really? What sort of things do you write?"

"Mostly fiction, but historical stuff based on truth. I love doing research, but I'm still a little green around the gills when it comes to writing," she admitted.

"Historical fiction, huh? That's incredible. What time period?"

Jana stood up and went to the fridge, bringing back a two-liter bottle of Pepsi. If we were anyone else, we'd probably be chatting over a bottle of wine. Or sharing beers on the patio.

But, alas, it was just the two of us and our bubbly Pepsis in glass cups.

"I'm interested in so many things, but right now I'm researching the reign of Henry the Eighth."

"Ah. Please excuse my ignorance, but all I know about that man is that he killed his wives. Wasn't he married to like eight different women?"

"Six, and he didn't kill them all," Jana said. "And you're exactly right. His tumultuous love life is what he's known for. But there are bigger repercussions than that. I find his wives to be the most interesting thing about him, and in particular, their individual fates."

"Tell me more," I said, chewing.

"Each woman could have been any of us, really; each wife one side of ourselves; each fate a lesson for girls everywhere. Don't be barren and boring like Catherine of Aragon. Don't be an adulteress like Anne Boleyn or Catherine Howard. Don't be sickly like Jane Seymour. Don't be ugly like Anne of Cleves or a feminist like Catherine Parr."

Jana's whole face came alive as she talked, smile lines splitting around her eyes. I could tell she was passionate and in her element when she talked about her writing research.

"Well, it sounds to me like Henry needed a Franken-wife —combine the qualities he loved about all of them into one, and then perchance he would have been satisfied a bit more," I teased.

Jana laughed, her bright blue eyes shining with delight.

"That's just it, isn't it? Therein lies the problem—none of us are perfect. We all have goodness inside us, and we're also equipped with our own unique flaws. Yet Henry himself was the most defective of them all."

"Men usually are," I muttered, stabbing at my pizza with a fork. Imagining Francis's stupid face. My thoughts drifted back to that old photograph in the basement, the one of him looking on at Sara, his face a mask of pure adoration. *What happened? And how did he become king of their castle?* I wondered.

"And most of the things he accused them of weren't even close to the truth," Jana continued. "Catherine of Aragon bore him a daughter. There was no proof the others were unfaithful or immoral. Yet they are remembered for their deaths and their reputations, not for who they really were."

"I know the feeling," I said. "It's like once you're branded, it never rubs off."

"If you're a woman, that is," Jana said, pointing her fork at me, then turning it slowly back at herself.

"Exactly."

We went on like that for hours, Jana finally offering to show me some of her finished pages. I'd known she was smart and kind, but I'd never realized how fascinating she was. She loved to read and talk, and I could almost imagine us like this every week, hanging out and chatting about God-knows-what during a regular girls' night.

Oh, how I long for that sort of normal in mine and Gemma's life, for a change.

After we boxed up the leftovers and cleared up the kitchen, I excused myself to make some calls.

"I'm going to follow up with my old boss and landlord," I said. "Is it okay if I go outside on the porch, to get some privacy?"

Jana waved me away. "You don't have to ask my permission for everything. This isn't jail or rehab. And it certainly isn't Francis's house. I won't send you to the Tower for disobeying me," she said.

"Off with her head," I said, slicing a finger across my neck.

Outside, I stepped off the porch and strolled down the deserted gravel driveway, trying to get as far out of earshot as possible. I did plan to call my boss and landlord, but I needed to take care of something else first while I had the chance.

I used my new phone to dial the number, one I hadn't called in ages.

When I heard the voice on the other end, I was almost

too surprised to respond. It sounded like the voice of a stranger.

I took a deep breath. "It's me. Norah," I spoke, softly. "I have a favor to ask and it's not like you can say you don't owe me..."

Chapter Twenty-Six

As Jana parked in front of Sara and Francis's eerie home, I felt a sense of desperation come over me. Sure, I was glad to be back with Gemma, but aside from that, I hated returning to this place. I was terrified of my uncle and aunt, but I was more afraid of leaving Gemma alone with them for much longer... *At least here I can have a better chance of protecting her.*

Big, open windows stared back at me like angry, bulging eyes. As though the whole awful house had come alive to greet me.

"Thanks again for letting me stay with you," I told Jana, and I meant it. I'd had time to get my thoughts straightened out. To make a plan, just as she had suggested. As much as I wanted to trust Jana with the details of my plan, I couldn't rely on anyone to keep my secrets safe. Not until I'd regained custody.

"Want me to walk you in?" Jana offered. I shook my head and tried out a shaky smile.

"Nah. I'm a big girl. But thank you."

"Speaking of big girls and the *Big Book*—want me to pick you up for AA on Tuesday? There's a meeting at the church at five. And if Francis tries to give you any shit about it, just shoot me a text and I'll call him myself."

"Yes, I definitely do. And I'll probably text you later anyways. Tell you how it's going."

"You better." Jana smiled.

"Jana? If I don't call or text you tomorrow, will you come by? I don't trust these people and I need a back-up. Even if he opens the door and says I can't come out to see you, insist upon it or call the police. Don't take no for an answer."

Jana nodded, solemnly. "Of course, you got it."

I climbed out, waving at her with trepidation.

As Jana pulled away, I took a second to compose myself. Smoothed my shirt and finger-combed my hair. *Head up. Shoulders back. Big, grateful smile. Let them think you're not convinced they're hiding bodies in the shed anymore.*

As I raised my fist to knock, the door swung open.

"Hi, I'm back." Smiling tightly, I was surprised to see Aunt Sara and not the dominant Uncle Francis hovering in the doorway.

"Oh, I'm so glad you're here," Sara waved me inside. I noticed her hair was shabby, her clothing slightly mismatched. She looked... frazzled, and a little confused.

"Sara, are you okay?" I said, following her through the sitting area into the kitchen.

"Just fine, dear. Francis left with Gemma. He should be back soon though…"

My heart dropped.

"Where did they go?" I asked, phony smile plastered on my face. *Play nice. Every action is important now. Surely, he wouldn't do anything to hurt Gemma, would he? It seems like he wants to possess her, not kill her… but how can I be so sure?*

My phony smile was tugging. Threatening to rip and tear at the corners of my mouth.

"She went to stay the night with Susie over at Merrill's house. Francis is just dropping her."

I forced out the words: "Oh, how nice. I'm sure they'll have the best time."

"We made a pie. It's rhubarb, I think. Would you like a piece now?" Sara offered.

I shook my head. It was late, and although I was "playing nice", I didn't think that required that I eat pie. I'd lost my appetite anyway. The only person I wanted to see was Gemma, not these awful people.

"Thank you, but I had a bite with Jana before I came. I think I'll shower and change my clothes, then work on my AA steps before I tuck in early. My new medication makes me sleepy," I lied.

Sara smiled. I wouldn't swear to it, but hers looked almost as fake as mine.

"Sure thing, Norah. I'm glad to have you back. Are you feeling better now? Getting your thoughts straight…?"

My smile faltered, but only briefly. "Oh, yes! Much better now. I talked with the doctors while I was in there and they adjusted my medication. Losing someone you love the way I did and finding his... body. That can do funny things to a person's mind. It's a post-traumatic stress thing. I'm sorry about all the drama I caused." It pained me to say it, to push this lie, but if I had to be a phony in order to get my daughter back, then that is exactly what I'd do.

Sara nodded. For a moment, I thought she might reach out to hug me, and if so, I'd have to fight off the urge to slap her away.

"I'm sorry you have to go through that. Losing someone you love is difficult. But we're here for you. And of course, we'll do everything we can to help with Gemma. She's such a delight to have around, truly she is."

"She definitely is that," I said, grimly. "Thanks for taking care of her, and for letting me come back after all the craziness, Sara."

"You bet." She rested a hand on my shoulder, held it there a beat too long. "Well, enjoy your shower and rest."

Upstairs, I flung my coat on the bed and tugged my shoes and socks off. Falling back on the unmade covers, I turned my head to the right—coming face to face with the suitcase I'd left behind.

Back on my feet, I went over and snapped it open. Searched for the incriminating items the police and doctors had mentioned. The suicide note. The hypodermic needle. Both were gone, but I'd expected that. Sara and Francis were probably keeping those for "evidence" that I was unfit, to show the judge when we went to court.

Sighing deeply, I gathered my bed clothes and went to take a bath. I was disappointed that Gemma wasn't here tonight, but then again, maybe it was a good thing. The further I could keep her from this house until we could get away, the better.

An hour later, feeling warm and fuzzy from my bath, I climbed under the sheets and took out my new disposable cell phone. I needed to ask Jana something, and I'd waited until I was away from her to ask it. *Better if she doesn't see my face and try to read what I'm thinking in person.*

I texted quickly:

Settling in. Gemma isn't here. Went to stay with her cousin for the night. Things are going okay. Reading the Big Book. Hey, you mentioned Patricia from AA and I think you said she'd been in the program for a while?? Do you think she would be a good option for a sponsor? Someone I can call when I'm having cravings? I was hoping you had her number so I could introduce myself and ask about sponsorship.

I lay on my back, gripping the phone to my chest, as I waited breathlessly for her answer. The truth was, I needed an excuse to talk to Patricia about her grandchild who ran away. I needed to be certain that she was in fact a runaway, and not a dead girl rotting in my uncle's shed. *Or wherever he moved that damn barrel to*, I thought, uneasily.

The phone vibrated against my chest. I couldn't help smiling as I read her response. I'd asked Jana for Patricia's phone number, but what I got was even better—Patricia's home address.

Chapter Twenty-Seven

Patricia's A-frame cottage was less homey than Jana's, but just as small. I took a shallow breath and knocked. When I'd mentioned meeting my sponsor, I'd half-expected Sara and Francis to say no, or, at the very least, insist on coming with me. But Sara had ushered me out of the house that morning, thrusting her car keys in my hand.

Now I was standing here at my future (hopefully) sponsor's door, hoping for her help in more ways than one.

Thankfully, Jana had phoned her first—doing me a huge favor, by giving her my background info. *She's more than willing to sponsor you*, Jana had told me. Which came as a relief to me. Not because I wanted a sponsor—although getting one probably wasn't a bad idea—but because I needed an excuse to see her. Needed to know if her granddaughter was the hideous, bloated face I'd seen in the barrel.

I needed answers. But also—I needed to know the truth

205

for myself. I wasn't crazy. I didn't imagine that face. *It has to belong to someone...*

I shuddered, just as the door creaked open before me.

Patricia was older than I'd expected, curly wig crooked on her head.

"H-hi there," I stammered. "I'm Norah. Jana said—"

"Yes, yes! Come on in, my sweets."

I smiled fondly, stepping inside her home with gratitude. I'd never been called "sweets" before.

The cottage was cold. Cheap, peeling paint adorned the walls. "This way," she said, motioning toward the kitchen. "Sorry for the mess," she added, clearing away a few sodden paper plates and napkins. "I had a gentleman friend over last night, and I didn't bother with the clean-up before we went to bed, if you catch my drift."

I coughed in my hand to hide a smile. "Yes, I think I do."

Patricia's refrigerator was covered in magnets and pictures. I wanted to stand up and get closer, examine every single face on them, but I didn't want to act like a weirdo.

"Soda okay?" she asked, opening the fridge door and reaching inside.

"Soda's perfect."

A few minutes later, we were sharing Cokes and sitting across from each other at the kitchen table.

"Ever had a sponsor before?"

I shook my head.

"Well, I'm glad you asked me then. I've been sober for eight years now. And before that, I was sober for twenty. I never thought I'd fall off the wagon when I did, but life throws curveballs sometimes… and, when you're an addict or an alcoholic, it's so easy to go back to what feels good and normal in terms of stress."

It wasn't until an hour later of listening to Patricia talk about her sober journey that I had a chance to ask about her granddaughter.

"If you don't mind me asking, what triggered your relapse? Jana mentioned something about your granddaughter going missing." It was bold of me to ask, and shitty to throw Jana under the bus, but I was desperate to get more answers.

If Patricia was put off by my question, she didn't show it.

"Willow, yes."

"That's a beautiful name," I said, quietly.

"Her mama picked it. It wouldn't have been my first choice, a little odd and unusual—but her mother never listened to me, anyway."

I nodded along, hoping she'd say more. But she didn't.

"The role of a sponsor is simple—to help you stay sober. When you're new in the program, with not a lot of sober days under your belt, the risk of relapse is high. Very high. I attend meetings three or four days a week. Fresh out of rehab, I'm going to recommend ninety meetings in ninety days. You need a support system. So, I'll swing by and pick you up for meetings if you need a ride. And yes, I drive just fine," she said, smiling at my raised eyebrows.

I blushed, nodding.

"Have you been having cravings?"

"No," I said, relieved to find that it was the truth. "In fact, just the thought of using makes my stomach turn. I have so many terrible memories, so much guilt…"

Patricia stared at me, pensively, fingers templed over her tattooed lip liner. I could tell she'd had a rougher life once, the frown lines around her mouth, the edge of a homemade tattoo peeking out from the corner of her short-sleeved sweater.

"That's good. But what happens when you come face to face with the drug, or another drug for that matter? The temptation to use doesn't seem like much, until an opportunity presents itself. And although it's nice to think we'll be smart enough to never put ourselves in that sort of position again, you never know when the opportunity will arise."

I thought about that day in the shed—the liquor bottles on the shelves. The fantasy of chugging the booze, numbing the pain and guilt that I carried like a concrete slab around my neck. I wasn't rough like Patricia on the outside, but inside… That was a whole other story.

"I'll give you my number. Feel free to call me day or night. I don't sleep much anymore. Everything wakes me up. If you want to use, and even if you're determined to do it, call me anyway. Give me a chance to change your mind, that's all I ask."

I nodded. "I hope that never happens, but if it does…"

"*When* it does," Patricia said, solemnly. "There will come a day when you'll be tested, truly tested. Don't let yourself think it isn't possible. It's not only possible, it's likely. If you got hooked one time, you can get hooked again."

She was right. More right than I cared to admit.

"Thank you for doing this, Patricia. Seriously. And I'd love to attend meetings with you," I said, my words genuine. Part of me almost wished I had a Patricia in Chicago. *I suppose when Gemma and I return home, I'll have to find a new sponsor as soon as I get there...*

The conversation was wrapping up, and I still didn't have the information I'd come for. Patricia stood and I stood too, a wave of disappointment rolling over me. *Ask her. Just do it.*

But we were moving, headed back for the door. My ingrained politeness and manners wouldn't allow me to straight-out ask this kind woman nosy questions such as: *what the hell happened to your granddaughter?*

"The most important thing right now is that I stay sober for my daughter, Gemma. I don't want to lose her. She's the only thing that matters to me," I said, words rushing out as we paused in the living room area.

Patricia reached out, gripping my elbows in her hands. "She deserves a mother who is sober. And I'm glad you're doing it for her. But first, you must do it for you. You must learn to be a happy, whole person without a crutch to lean on."

"You're right," I said, choking back tears. The thought of losing Gemma was too much. But the thought of losing myself... going back to being that person, that soulless, miserable person... I couldn't do that either. *I won't let myself go back to that. I won't suffer the same fate as Finn.*

"That's my granddaughter, Willow."

I jerked my head over to where she was pointing. A small, gold-framed photograph sat next to an oak entertainment center. I moved closer, chest filled with dread.

Willow was a lovely girl. It was a school photograph, that was obvious. Willow was posed, one hand curled into a fist propped under her chin, her school's name in big blocky letters on the floor beside her.

She's not the girl in the barrel. I felt a mixture of relief, and something else—frustration, at still not knowing who the woman was. And fear that maybe the doctors were right—it was an acute stress reaction; I saw a dead body instead of rotting fruit because I'd recently found my fiancé bloody and lifeless...

Was it possible I'd imagined it? According to the doctors at the inpatient clinic, the answer was yes. I went to that shed searching for answers, a reason not to trust my uncle. And then I saw the booze, and thought about Finn, dead and bleeding on the floor... and in my mind, I saw the worst possible outcome when I flipped the lid on that barrel...

"What happened to her?" I asked, rocks in my throat. Patricia was staring at the photo, eyes watery and strange. My heart broke for her, and I couldn't help imagining what I would do if I lost my Gemma.

"I raised her after her mama left. I was supposed to be

better, you know? Her mom was hooked on crank, her dad long gone from the picture… and here I was, the grandma who could rectify everything."

I watched her face, understanding the guilt and shame written across it.

"But that's the thing about addiction. It doesn't usually spring out of nowhere. I was a drunk when my daughter Tanya was growing up, and I was still a drunk when she gave birth to Willow. But sometimes a drunk can hide it better than a junkie, you know? I was a high-functioning alcoholic, keeping a job and driving. You'd never know I was drinking. But Willow knew. She saw me shit-faced every night, even though I tried to hide it. She said I reminded her of her mother. It killed me when she said that, but at the same time, I loved my Tanya too. Her using was my fault. It all was. But that's something I have to live with. Tanya ran off and Willow ran off too. I have to live with my mistakes; we all do."

My eyes traveled from Willow's photo to the others around the room.

"Do you think she'll come back?" I asked, walking over to a younger photo of Willow. In this one, she was straddling a Huffy bike, equipped with a basket and horn. The big smile on her face hid the fact that she grew up with an addicted mother, absent father, and alcoholic grandmother.

"I hope not," Patricia said, solemnly.

When I gave her a questioning look, she said, "Willow isn't missing, honey. She still contacts me from time to time.

She's living in Denver now with her girlfriend. Getting ready to go to college. I won't ask her to come back to me."

The fact that she had talked to her granddaughter erased my fears that she was dead in a barrel somewhere, either at the hands of Uncle Francis or someone else.

"I'm glad she's doing well. You must have done something right," I said, with a smile.

But if Patricia heard my encouraging words, she didn't let on. I followed her gaze to where she was looking, another set of photographs on the wall. Soundlessly, I walked over to the photo in the center, squinting to see through the glare of a dusty beam of sunlight coming from the window.

The woman in this photo was older and taller than Willow, her eyes bright and her hair midnight black. She looked nothing like her daughter or her mother.

"That's my Tanya. She took off too and unlike my granddaughter, she doesn't stay in touch. She's beautiful, isn't she?"

"Yes," I said, reaching out a finger to wipe dust from the glass over her face. "She certainly is."

"Haven't seen or heard from her in a long time. I pray she's not out on the streets somewhere, still using, but it's possible. I pray for her every night," Patricia said.

"Thank you for being my sponsor and for sharing so much with me," I said. "I have to get back to my aunt and uncle's now, but I'll call you soon."

"Please do," Patricia said, seeing me out the front door.

I rushed through it, making a beeline for Sara's Taurus. I

didn't look back as I climbed in the car, but I could feel Patricia watching, still standing there, stooped over at the door.

I waited until I was out of the driveway and about a mile down the road before I pulled over. Laying my head against the steering wheel, I let the tears come freely.

Oh God. That poor woman. What am I going to do?

Because she was right about one thing—her granddaughter was gone, off to a better place and a brighter future. But her daughter... those eyes and lips, that hair... *I know that face.* I didn't imagine that body I saw.

Patricia's daughter, Tanya, no longer had a future. Tanya was dead, her body decaying somewhere—somewhere in my uncle's barrel, wherever he'd moved it to.

Chapter Twenty-Eight

I didn't remember leaving Patricia's house, or the windy, long drive back to my uncle's home. What I did remember: the dark waves of hair, like slimy black strings. Bright eyes attached to a ghostly white face, bulging from their sockets. Sagging flesh, mottled and gray, falling from the bone…

It was her. A rotten, decaying version of her. But it was definitely her—not Patricia's granddaughter, Willow, but the mother who came before her, Tanya.

Why? Why would Francis keep her body in his shed? And, although I couldn't prove he'd done it—why had he killed her?

A love affair gone wrong? Some sort of accidental death he wanted to cover up…?

Nothing made sense anymore.

My hands were shaking so hard, I had to grip the wheel to keep them steady. I tried to focus on the road, but my world was spinning. The yellow lines doubling, the forest of trees whispering by in a blur of confusion.

What am I supposed to do now? What can I do?

I imagined myself turning back around, saddling up to Patricia's door again. Telling her the honest truth, ripping the Band-aid off.

But the body is gone, the barrel replaced with a rotten mixture of alcohol and fruit, supposedly.

Thoughts whirring in every direction, I considered something I hadn't before—*what if the officer is covering for him for some reason? Claiming he found something else when he in fact saw the same putrid corpse that I did?*

Shaking my head, I tried to dispel that idea. No decent cop in their right mind would cover up something like that, no matter how well known or well-liked Francis was in town.

He doesn't seem particularly likable, if you ask me. I can't see anyone covering up a murder for him.

One thing I'd learned about memory—it isn't always reliable. But sometimes, over time, bits and pieces *do* come back. Like that night with Finn, it took days—weeks, even—for the whole traumatic event to come back in full color. Even now, there were still little details I was probably forgetting...

I closed my eyes briefly, Sara's Taurus swaying side to side on the road. In my mind, I was moving through the forest, raising the hammer to smash the lock off my uncle's shed.

I opened my eyes. Blinked.

Then what? Think, Norah, think! Try to remember every minute detail. Something that might be important. Something you can use to prove your accusation was true.

Because this was no longer just about me, my daughter... Patricia's daughter deserved justice, too. If Tanya was gone, her body stuffed away like that. her mother deserved to know about it.

Closing my eyes again, I kept moving through my mind. Retracing the steps.

I approached the rows of alcohol on the shelves. Saw the Everclear. Was shaken by memories of Finn. I was tempted to take the bottle, lift it to my lips... but I put the cap back on.

I didn't do it.

I decided to leave, feeling foolish. Regretful. Panicked about what I'd done. And that's when I stubbed my toe on the barrel. That's when I stopped to consider its possible contents.

I opened the lid, a short grueling process, and that's when I saw... when I saw...

Wait, back up a minute.

The barrel was gray, with a rusty orange tint to it. It was old, fading... but there were letters. Definitely letters on the front of it.

What were the words on the barrel? Did I even really look?

I squeezed my eyes shut, let the wheel slip away from my palms. And the words came floating back to me, as though they'd never left in the first place: *Jones Meat Solutions.*

My eyes flew open, a short intake of breath, and I swerved back into my lane with a screeching of tires.

Jones Meat Solutions. *What the hell does that mean?*

Sara had mentioned Uncle Francis's job—he worked at the cement factory. *Is that where he got the barrel? If so, what's the association with this Meat Solutions place?*

It had to be some sort of local company. A place where he got the barrel, or a possible accomplice?

I was close to home. *Too close.*

Impulsively, I whipped the car over to the emergency lane and threw on the brake. Taking my phone out, I sent a quick text to Jana. If anyone could tell me more about this town and the people in it, it was her.

I could see Jana writing, typing back a response.

"Come on," I whined, looking out my side and rearview mirrors. Checking for passing cars. I could almost imagine Francis pulling up beside me. Demanding to know what I was doing, who I was speaking to.

When the phone dinged, I snapped it up eagerly. *Please know something that can help me, Jana. I need to figure this out, get my daughter away from these creeps…*

I know the place. It's a poultry-processing plant. Why? What's going on? You got some chickens you need butchered, or what?

My stomach curled at the word "butchered".

I ignored her questions and wrote:

Where's it at, do you know?

Jana's response was immediate:

It's super close to you, actually. Only a few miles from your aunt's place. Near Evergreen and Birch. You OK? Talk to me.

Once again, I ignored Jana's question, putting the car back into gear.

Chapter Twenty-Nine

I made a left on Evergreen, then a right on Birch. I could smell the poultry plant before I saw it. Something sweet and chemical-ish, not wholly unpleasant.

A gravel driveway led to a metal gate; a peeling green sign that read *Meat Solutions* was nailed to a cracked post in the grass. I assumed it belonged to Jones Meat Solutions. *How many meat solutions does one town need?*

The gate was unlocked, barely nudged open. I parked the Taurus there and got out, shivering from the cold. A storm was brewing, low-slung clouds evolving into fat, bulging bruises that gathered over the tree line.

Slipping through the unlocked gate, I crossed an overgrown field just as fat droplets of rain came pouring down. A long aluminum building with the same logo I'd seen on the barrel was set before me.

It's no surprise that the barrel came from here, since it's practically my uncle's neighbor.

221

The stench in the air was overpowering, and not what I'd expected—it was the pungent aroma of ammonia. The closer I got, the queasier I became.

I flung open the door, escaping from the rain. I gasped when I turned and got a good look around the plant.

There were birds on the ceiling, hanging by their feet, moving along an assembly line of metal machines. I stared at the dead animals, mouth agape.

"What the hell are you doing in here?"

I yelped, turning toward the voice. It came from an older gentleman, short and skinny. He came striding toward me, a look of fear on his face.

"Are you here to inspect or something?" he asked, stopped a few inches away. Up close, I could tell he was younger than I'd originally thought; only, his skin was over-tanned and wrinkly, stretched tight across his bones. I noticed that he was a fellow weary traveler—if not worn down by drugs or the drink, by life in general.

"No. I-I…" I stammered, struggling to come up with an excuse, only now realizing I hadn't planned out anything. "I'm Norah. I live down the road, with Sara and Francis Bancroft."

"Ah. Okay." The man raised his eyebrows, not looking convinced.

Thunder boomed outside, making the whole building shake. I looked around the poultry plant uneasily—there were no workers in sight, just lots of machines. *If this man killed Patricia's daughter and stuffed her in one of his barrels, then I'm the dumbest person on earth for walking right into the path of a killer.*

"I'm Tim. This is my place. Are Francis or Sara having some sort of trouble?"

"No, nothing like that." *So, he definitely knows my aunt and uncle then.*

"I was wondering if you're hiring. I'm new to town." It was a stupid lie, but I needed something to soften the edges of my suspicious visit. *This could all backfire on me. He could call Francis as soon as I leave here, and tell him I came by...*

"Not hiring right now, but maybe in the future," Tim said, scratching his chin and looking over at his dead chicken meat, uncomfortably.

"Oh. Okay. Well, let me know. I don't have any experience with this sort of thing, but I've worked in lots of restaurants. I love chicken."

I love chicken. I closed my eyes, wishing I weren't so awkward when I was nervous.

"How's your aunt and uncle?" Tim reached into his T-shirt pocket, dug around for a pack of smokes.

"They're doing well. They're helping me out with my daughter while I get back on my feet."

Tim paused, looking at me in a different way. Something in his eyes I couldn't quite read...

"Care if we step out for a second? I need a smoke."

"Of course not," I said, relieved to escape the pungent smells and the nasty sight of those birds.

I watched as he walked over to a row of switches on the wall. There was a loud whooshing sound, and something on the belt stopped. I tried not to look at the batch of chickens closest to me. Their heads had just been severed by some sort of metal cutting machine.

I shivered, wrapping my arms around myself.

Tim walked out through the front door, and I followed closely behind. As I watched him light up his cigarette, sucking in the abrasive smoke, I yearned for my electronic cigarette. It was back home at the house, still tucked away in my suitcase.

"You said they're helping out with your daughter, huh? That's great."

I nodded. I was unsure what to do with my hands, so I tucked them in my pockets. The rain was coming down in sheets, and I clung to the side of the building, staying dry beneath the protective awning.

"How do you know my uncle? Are you friends?"

Tim took a long drag on his cigarette, staring into the rain. He was quiet. For the first time, I had an opportunity to really study his face. He looked strangely familiar.

"I usually come by a few times a year and bring them some meat." He waved his hand at the plant behind him.

"That's awfully nice of you."

"It's nothing compared to what I owe them."

Now my interest was piqued. "Why would you owe them?"

Again, there was silence—several beats too long. I wished again for my cigarette and considered asking to bum one.

"It was a long time ago. I was young then, better-looking than I am now." Tim laughed, his chuckles evolving to a wet cough. I waited for him to compose himself.

"What happened?"

"Your aunt and uncle helped me out one time when I needed them." He tossed out his cigarette, reaching for another.

I couldn't help asking. "Did they help out with your daughter Constance?" There was no denying it; he was a spitting image of the little girl in the photographs. The one I thought I used to play with in the garden, and the one who owned the doll house in the sealed-off room...

Tim frowned. "Why are you asking about Connie? Did you know her or something?"

Connie. Now there's something more familiar.

"I think I played with Connie a few times when I was little. I visited Aunt Sara when I was a child and I have memories of a little girl..."

Tim's face was stiff, unreadable. Finally, he spoke. "That makes sense, I guess. You look about her age."

"Does she still live around here?" I asked, holding my breath. Expecting the worst.

Tim launched his half-smoked cigarette with a flick of his wrist, his expression hardening.

"I don't know why you're asking so many questions. I would have thought a niece of Francis and Sara's might have a little more couth. Connie's mother was hooked on crank, okay? I never used, but I drank, and I was about to go away for a B&E charge right after she was born."

I waited, watching his face. There was guilt written all over it.

"Sara and Francis offered to take her for us. They couldn't have kids of their own. Well, I'm sure you already know that. And they just adored her. Connie was a tiny blonde angel, energetic and happy. You'd never know she came from two godawful parents like me and Luanda. So, they took her in. Gave her a home. And I went off to serve my time. Things were good for a little while, at least for Connie. She seemed happy there at the farmhouse with your aunt and uncle..."

"What changed?" I felt a chill at the base of my spine, working its way up my backside. *What did Francis do to this poor man's daughter?*

"Lu came back to town a few months before I was getting released. After all those years, she said she was clean. Wanted Connie back even though Connie didn't know her mama at all. We didn't have a formal arrangement, nothing like that. So, Sara and Francis had no choice but to let her go. Lu was her biological mother. She had more rights than any of us."

"I'm sorry. Did you lose contact...?"

Tim turned around, as though he were going to walk away, back inside the building and away from this conversation. He ran his hands through his hair. I'd pushed this strange man way too far and he was done talking.

But then he stopped, back turned to me.

"Lu moved away with Connie. Took her out to Wisconsin. She met a boyfriend there. Probably relapsed pretty fast. But that's how the story goes with junkies, doesn't it?"

I wanted to defend myself, insist that: *No. Some of us do get clean and stay clean.*

But I kept my mouth shut. This man's pain was in the air, throbbing and palpable.

I thought he was done talking, but he wasn't. He turned back around to look at me, eyes hard and black as marbles.

"I never saw Connie again. And your aunt and uncle were devastated that she was gone. I'm sure she's out there somewhere, hopefully still alive. But with her junkie mother in charge, there's no telling what happened."

"I'm so sorry." It sounded stupid, pointless, coming from my mouth.

"Don't be sorry. Just take care of your kid. And if your aunt and uncle are helping you out, then you should feel grateful."

Chapter Thirty

STEP 9: FORGIVENESS

I gnawed on the flesh of my inner cheek, an anxious tic I didn't remember having until now, as I drove back to my aunt and uncle's home. The Taurus moved slowly, few cars on the road, barely reaching thirty miles per hour as I tried to process the stories of Patricia Belfry and Tim Jones. The stories of little Constance and Tanya, and so many other girls and women like them.

My brain was moving on autopilot, moving in the opposite direction of my aunt and uncle's home...

Francis and Sara took in a little girl. But then her addicted mother came back and skipped town with her... Is that why they're so hateful toward me? I remind them of Connie's junkie mother, and Gemma reminds them of the girl they once cared for...?

This still gave me no more clues about why Francis killed Tanya and stuffed her in a barrel. *How is she related to all this?*

There was a theme here though—one I couldn't seem to get away from. A theme, playing over and over in my head, like the worst soundtrack of my life. The track on a loop, endless repetition.

Mothers and daughters. Addiction. Mistakes that can't be undone. Unforgiven.

What will I do to protect my own daughter? Make sure that no one hurts her—including me.

I was in another place, another world, so much so that I nearly passed by the creepy monster house on the hill belonging to my aunt and uncle.

Slamming on the brakes, I threw the car in reverse, and backed up into the driveway. It was then that I saw them in my rearview mirror. Francis and another man, huddled close together, talking animatedly on the porch.

I put the car in park and stepped out. I wasn't in the mood for Francis's shit.

Isn't he supposed to be at work? And who's he talking to?

Francis stood with his big beefy arms wrapped around himself, glaring at the man. The man in the suit with the cheap gold chain.

When the man turned to look at me, I couldn't help but smile, warily. *Neil knows how to make a deal*—his corny catchphrase from the radio playing on a loop in my brain.

His commercials were underwhelming, and that was putting it mildly. But Neil "The Deal" Benson was the only lawyer within a hundred miles who agreed to take on my case for a retainer of less than $300.

A bad lawyer is better than no lawyer at all. You should show up with someone, Jana had told me.

"Norah, there you are!" Neil stuck out his hand and I took it, then glanced over at Francis for a reaction. His jaw was set in a grim line, eyes full-black with anger.

Francis, meet my lawyer. You're not the only one with tricks up your sleeve. He might not be top-of-the-line, but I have a contingency plan too.

"If you don't mind, sir, I need to speak with my client in private," Neil said. He shot a ferocious grin in Francis's direction and pointed double finger guns at me.

Chapter Thirty-One

With court less than twenty-four hours away, I found that I could barely sleep. My appetite was all but gone. Gemma was spending more and more time away from the house, with Merrill and Susie. Part of me hated that, and the other part... The other part was relieved. *I don't trust these people and the farther she is from here, the better. But then again, what do I know about Merrill, really?*

Perhaps I can't trust her either.

Patricia was waiting for me in the driveway, her black Buick old but shiny, and well cared for. As I climbed in the passenger's side, Francis watched from the window. Patricia raised her hand, wiggled her fingers in greeting at him.

"Silly old buzzard," she huffed, smiling over at me.

I forced myself to smile back. Truth was, I could barely face her... not after knowing what I thought I knew about her daughter. But over the last couple days, I'd started to doubt myself again. The image of the girl in the barrel was growing less and less pronounced... I kept picturing a lumpy rotten stew of fruit, the boozy scent of alcohol stinging my nostrils replacing the sharp smell of death.

"You all right?" Patricia turned up the radio. Patsy Cline. Somehow it suited her. My mother used to like Patsy too.

"I'm okay, I guess. Worried about court."

We were on our way to an AA meeting, my second one this week, and I looked forward to seeing Jana too. In the dingy church basement bathroom, she had watched me take my piss test at our last meeting. Afterwards, we had saved the results and snapped photos.

More evidence for my lawyer.

He had assured me the case was simple. We had a letter from my old boss, assuring my position was still being held for me when Gemma and I returned to Chicago. And, thankfully, my landlord, as sketchy as he could be sometimes, had faxed over a letter on my behalf, about my rental agreement.

I will have employment and a place to live. My drug screens are all clear. They have no reason not to give my daughter back to me tomorrow.

But that wasn't exactly true—I knew that Francis would use my past to hurt me: the history contained in the discharge papers I'd so readily handed over, and recent events, calling the cops for "no reason", my supposed "stress reaction" in the shed, as well as the suicide note, and the old needle hidden inside my suitcase.

Francis would do everything to keep my daughter. And Sara would go along with anything Francis did, like the good little puppet she was. Because they didn't want to lose another little girl to her addicted mother... like they did with Connie.

Perhaps my situation with Gemma is triggering an "acute stress reaction" in them, I thought, remembering the therapist's garbled explanation for the body I thought I saw in the barrel. Regardless, Gemma was my daughter and she needed to stay with me. I didn't trust Francis or Sara, and as much as I wanted to feel sorry for them, and for Tim, over losing Constance... I had to focus on protecting my own right now.

"I know you're worried, but is there something else? You're in a whole other world, right now, and I'm your sponsor. You're supposed to be talking to me," Patricia said, parking the boat of a Buick in front of the church. Our meetings were held on the backside, down in the church basement. It was dark and dreary, and the subject matter inside wasn't much better, but it felt like home when I was with Jana and Patricia.

"I will talk if I need to, I promise. I'm just glad to be here today." I motioned at the church.

And it was true. The group was small, fewer than ten of us and mostly women. The coffee sucked and the donuts were stale, but it was nice being around other people who knew what it was like to lose everything, and who weren't judging you for it, at least not judging you in a mean way.

"Well, let's get going. Jana brought another test for you to take. Your last one before court tomorrow," Patricia said.

We climbed out of the car, an icy blast of wind sneaking through my clothes, making me shiver from head to toe. I'd miss the meetings when I went back to Chicago. And I'd miss Patricia and Jana. But I wouldn't miss this hellish town. And I certainly wouldn't miss that creepy old house I'd been forced to stay in.

Chapter Thirty-Two

The courtroom was empty. Not like the courtrooms you see on TV, where the gallery is full of angry, gaping spectators.

I took a seat at the defendant's table, picking stray hairs off the front of my dress. I'd borrowed it from Jana since the only dress I owned was ragged and faded. Even though it was a little snug around my hips, it looked nicer than what I was used to.

Like a live wire, my nerves had come alive. I was jittery, my ears ringing. Like last time when I was in court, I got the strange sensation that my brain was disconnected from my body.

Neil "The Deal" Benson stood over at the prosecutor's table, talking it up. It worried me, the way they almost acted like they knew each other. As though they were old college chums.

Finally, he turned his head, eyes connecting with mine. I looked away, focusing back on my dress and my shaky hands in my lap. I was relying on this guy to come through for me, even though he was the last person I should have trusted.

Please let him do a good job today. I need my daughter back...

"Don't worry. We're all friendly around here," Neil said, taking a seat at the table beside me. "It's a lawyer thing. We cut the shit and we act like best buddies outside the courtroom, but when it comes to the law and fighting for our clients... we're cold as ice, believe it or not." He held up one fist and pumped it in the air.

"I believe you," I said, rolling my eyes.

The door to the courtroom squeaked open. From the corner of my eye, I watched Francis and Sara enter the room and make a beeline for the front row.

Seconds later, the door flew open again. I didn't turn my head until my lawyer whispered, "Do you know who that is, Norah?"

I turned my head, slowly, thoughts far away and focused on my new fantasy life with Gemma. Back in our own apartment, far away from my controlling relatives and that dusty house... the barrel...

My mouth fell open when I saw her. Small and petite, cute hair that ended at her chin... She smiled over at Francis and Sara, then took a seat in the back of the courtroom. A few more stragglers came pouring in, but I was facing forward. *Frozen in fear.*

"I don't know who she is," I said. It was true—I didn't know her. Never spoke to her a day in my life.

But that didn't mean I didn't recognize her. I had no doubt—she was the woman in the garden, the one I'd spotted sneaking around with Francis at night.

Chapter Thirty-Three

My lawyer's lips were moving but I could barely hear him. Ears still ringing, my whole body was ringing too. I had a feeling in my gut; one I couldn't shake. *Something is about to go wrong. Even though I don't know who this mystery woman is, I sure as hell recognize her.*

I followed my lawyer with my eyes as he approached the bench, handing over a stack of papers. *Proof of my future employment and housing. My clean drug screens.*

The judge was a large man, almost reminding me of Francis, but his hair was silver, his skin tanned as though he'd just come home from a tropical vacation. He looked like a serious man, giving nothing away. The perfect poker face. *What is he thinking?* I wondered. *And how bizarre is it that this man—this stranger with his silly tan—gets to decide the fate of my daughter? Gets to change our lives so significantly, for better or worse? What makes him so special that he gets to hold that much control over my and my daughter's future?*

The judge looked at the papers in front of him and glanced over at me, then his eyes traveled over to Francis and Sara. I looked too. They were strangely calm. Francis's hands were resting neatly on his lap in front of him; Sara was so small beside his massive form that I could barely see her tiny body.

The prosecutor was on his feet now, also approaching the bench. Moments later, I watched, as he pointed toward the courtroom. Past my aunt and uncle and me, toward the strange woman, one of only a few spectators in the gallery.

Patricia and Jana had offered to come, but they'd already written letters for me for the court, so it had seemed unnecessary. But now, I almost wished I had asked them. *Is there anyone in this room who is really on my side?*

There is. But I don't want to use my contingency plan if I don't have to.

"Miss Akers, please approach the bench," the judge said.

Akers. There's nothing familiar about that name.

The mystery woman took her time, her pantsuit pretty but rumpled, too large for her frame. She took a seat in the witness box.

My throat was dry, no saliva left, and I wished for a cup of water. *Or a stiff drink to take the edge off,* I thought, impulsively.

The moment her mouth was moving, my mind was spinning... trying to play catch-up with her words.

"Norah came into the liquor store where I worked a few days ago. She bought tiny shots of vodka, then asked if I knew who the local hook-up was. She was looking for heroin," the stranger said. Her eyes were cast straight ahead, refusing to look me in the face.

If you're going to tell a bold-faced lie, at least have the guts to face me.

I wanted to stand up and scream. If this were a movie, I probably would have. But I was frozen in my chair, unable to move. Unable to defend myself.

My lawyer was back over by my side in an instant. I tried to focus on his tie, the whirly pattern of stripes. *Don't panic don't panic don't panic.*

"A moment with my client please," he told the judge.

The room was frozen, that lying bitch still planted on the stand. *"Plant" is a good word for her. That, or phony or fraud.*

The judge watched us with steepled fingers. And although I didn't dare look at my aunt and uncle, I could imagine them watching too.

"I don't know that woman. Her story is completely untrue," I whispered to Neil.

"Are you sure?" he asked me. "Because she's willing to swear to it, under penalty of perjury."

"I think my uncle blackmailed her, or something. Maybe paid her off to do this. Or maybe they're having an affair. You see, I saw them late at night in the garden, whispering, right after I came to stay with them..."

"I thought you said you'd never seen her before..."

I groaned, loud enough to catch the judge's attention. "Well, I saw her once with my uncle in the back yard, creeping around like ghouls, talking in the dark of night... but I never went to the liquor store she works at, like she's claiming. In fact, I don't even know where the liquor store is in this town! And I'm clean. My drug screens prove that!" I shout-whispered.

I stared at the woman on the stand. She was smiling, showing all her teeth.

"Please. You have to do something. This is a do or die moment here." I turned around in my seat, scanning the courtroom. My eyes landed on my Plan B in the back row. I gave a nod and turned back around.

My lawyer and the prosecutor both approached the bench. Papers were shuffled and words were murmured. I thought I even heard a laugh, like they were part of some good old boys' club I'd never be a member of.

When my lawyer took his seat, he didn't even spare me a glance.

The judge cleared his throat, all heads turning his way.

"Although it appears to me that you're getting your life back on the right track, Miss Campbell, I do think there's still work to do. You're obviously still at risk when it comes to relapse. And with the recent events and your seventy-two-hour hospitalization, I'm inclined to believe that it's best for your daughter to stay with alternative family for a little while longer. Lucky for you, Francis and Sara have been kind enough to let you stay with them as well. They're under no obligation to allow that... and you still get to see your daughter this way."

"No no no no..." I said, shaking my head back and forth. I looked over at Neil again, eyes desperate. He gave a sorry expression and a small shrug. *Stupid man in a stupid suit... he was useless.*

"At least you still get to see her. And we can come back in a month or two..." he whispered.

No. I can't leave her with them. Hallucination or not, I can't take the risk... I have to get her away from Francis!

I turned around in my seat, eyes pleading. *Do something. For once in your life, do something to help me.*

The man in the gallery nodded, then got to his feet. *Plan B. The plan I never wanted to use.*

"Your Honor, before you make your decision... there's something I'd like to say," the tall, handsome gentleman from the back row called out.

The judge waved him forward, and I closed my eyes as he took the stand.

"Your honor, my name is Allen Greer and I'm the child's biological father. I'm more than willing to take Gemma in until my... excuse me, until Norah is deemed fit to do so."

Chapter Thirty-Four

O ver the years, Allen had reached out on several occasions. Offering financial support that I refused to take. Asking about our daughter.

His fancy dreams and his fancy life had paid off well for him. He'd finished first in his class, graduating from law school just as Gemma was celebrating her fifth birthday. I waited tables for pocket change, and he racked in the big bucks, representing big name company interests with his fancy law degree that he chose to pursue over fatherhood.

When I'd called him, asking him to come, it had been in a moment of desperation. I hadn't expected him to say yes. And I certainly hadn't expected this.

My lawyer was angry, huffing and puffing on his way out of the courtroom. "You are supposed to tell me these things... file the proper paperwork," he had scolded.

Ignoring both him and my relatives, I followed my ex

and daughter's biological father to where his fancy BMW was parked at the side of the courthouse.

"Let's talk in here. We'll have more privacy," Allen said, opening the passenger's door for me. *It's a little late for chivalry*, I wanted to tell him. But, despite all my resentment over the past, he had shown up today. I had to hold back some of my anger, at least for a little while.

After I was settled in the seat with the door closed, I slipped off my uncomfortable black dress shoes and laid my head sulkily on the seat rest. I couldn't help feeling anxious —yes, Gemma's father was back and willing to take temporary custody. But would the judge go for that? And was this really better than Francis and Sara?

Yes, it's better than a potential murderer, I decided.

"The DNA results should be back in a couple days," Allen said, resting a gentle hand on my arm. "And with my income and background, they can't refuse to give me my daughter. I have the means to take care of her until... well, until the judge says you can take her back. Plus, I'm closer to you than your relatives. I live right in Chicago, not too far from Gemma's old school district."

Allen lived in Wheaton, according to his website and social media accounts; not far at all from our apartment in Chicago. It was the perfect solution to get her out from under the thumb of Francis and Sara, but it didn't feel like a great choice either. Gemma didn't even know her father... and she'd already gone through so much.

Small mistakes that eventually led to huge ones... and here we were, paying dearly the price of my errors. It wasn't me I was worried about—it was Gemma. I deserved any and all punishment, but she sure as hell didn't. She deserved a steady, dramatic-free life.

"I know what you're thinking. You're worried about Gemma and you're afraid the judge won't let me take her over Francis and Sara. But I'm a lawyer, Norah! And I'm certain that they *will* grant me custody. I'm her father, with no arrest record and no history of issues of any kind... I make good money and I have a big house..."

"No issues, huh?"

That's what got under my craw—*that right there*. Suddenly, I was vilified for my mental health issues and my struggle with addiction. Yet here was Allen with a free pass —even though he'd run off and left us, never doing anything right by his daughter. Somehow, *he* was going to be deemed the worthy parent.

Nothing right by his daughter until now, I considered. *He's trying to help now...*

"I don't deserve to be in her life. I know that, Norah."

I was staring out the window of his fancy car, wishing to be anywhere but here. I wanted to get away from him... but there was nowhere to go but back to the house with Sara and Francis. *There are moments when I just want to crawl out of my own skin, shed it all like a snake...*

"You don't deserve her. She's a great girl, you know? She's smart and kind. Funny as hell. And she looks like me! You haven't done anything, anything at all..."

I was shocked to discover that I was sobbing, thick tears

tearing down my cheeks, leaking through my fingers as I tried to hide them.

"You're right about that. I don't. It should be me in there, being chastised for my behavior; not you."

"Damn right," I snapped, glancing over at him briefly. I wiped the tears from my face with the back of Jana's dress sleeve, looking at his stupid fancy suit. I hated myself for crying in front of him. Hated myself for allowing things to get to this.

"I do appreciate you coming though. She cannot stay with them. It's not safe for her, I feel it in my bones…"

But the thought of springing this on her now, introducing her to her father… I cringed at the thought.

Gemma knew she had a father named Allen. I'd even told her once that he was a successful lawyer. I told her that he was too busy with his career and made the dumb choice not to be a better father. I simply told her the truth. I didn't want her to think she'd done anything wrong; anything to make him vanish from her life. And I always played it up like he was someone important, someone doing something special in the world…

"I know there's no excuse for what I did. I was young and ignorant. Selfish as hell. And my father was pressuring me, riding my ass to go to college. There hasn't been a day gone by that I haven't wondered about you two. I look at your pictures all the time, the ones I can see that are public on Facebook. And you're right, Norah. She looks just like you. I know you made some mistakes recently, but you were young when you had her too. You're a good mom; I know you are. And I'm sorry I wasn't there to help you. I'm begging you to give me a second chance. Maybe not a permanent place in your lives, but at least this... something temporary until we can get back to Illinois. Please let me do this. Let me redeem myself in some small way here. For Gemma's sake. Just until the judge gives her back to you. Please."

I looked at him, really looked, seeing him for the first since he'd come back in my life, taking in all of his features. He wasn't that young, cocky guy anymore. His hair was graying prematurely at the temples and he had put on twenty or thirty pounds. His face was softer, kinder.

"She has your stupid nose," I said, sniffling.

His eyes watering with tears, he said, "You think so?"

I nodded, trying to swallow down the lump in my throat.

"Thank you. Not for fucking me over and leaving me behind. But thank you for doing this. For today. I hope the judge says yes, I really do."

"He will," Allen said, with confidence. "You just have to hold on for a couple more days until the results come in, and we'll get this all straightened out."

God, I pray he's right.

"It's going to be horrible. Going back to their house. They literally bribed someone to give false testimony against me. Who the hell does something like that?" I said, more to myself than him.

"I would say you could stay at the Holiday Inn with me,

but it's not suitable for anyone. I swear I think there's bed bugs," Allen grimaced.

"Serves you right," I said. I tried to say it as a joke, but the laughter died in my throat. Would I ever be able to laugh again? To feel at ease, not in fear for my daughter's safety…?

"Are you going back there?" Allen asked.

"My friend Jana said I could stay with her until we have the judge's answer, but I can't leave Gemma alone with them, no way. I want to make sure she's safe until we can get her with you. And then, eventually back with me," I said, focused on that last part.

"Absolutely. Just stay out of their paths while you're there and keep your head down for the next couple days until I hear back from the judge," Allen said.

That I could do. *No more questions or lurking around. I just want my daughter back. Everything else be damned. How will I go back to that house and look those liars—possible murderers— in the eye after the shit they pulled today?!*

The thought of it made my stomach turn.

I gave Allen one last glance before stepping out of the car. Like me, he had made a massive mistake. One he could never take back.

But if I consider myself deserving of a second chance with Gemma, then maybe he deserves one too.

Chapter Thirty-Five

STEP 10: MAINTENANCE

The house was quiet when I went inside, the only sounds the refrigerator humming, the whir of the air conditioner, the steady tick of the grandfather clock.

I found them sitting at the dining room table. Their expressions were blank, giving nothing away.

"I'm sorry things didn't go as you planned," I said, struggling to keep my voice steady. *They are supposed to be family. People I can lean on and trust. But they are so far from that... and even though I want to scream in their faces, I must stay calm for Gemma.*

"You're sorry?" The look Francis gave me said everything I needed to know—*he hates me. Always has. They never planned on relinquishing control of my daughter. They don't want to give her up the way they had to with Connie...*

"Allen is her biological father. And it's not like you can't still see her... We can visit, or you could come..." But of course I was lying. The moment I escaped this hellish house and my weirdo relatives, I planned on never looking back...

"Is Gemma still with Merrill? I want to talk to her when she gets back. Explain it to her... make sure she's okay with this..."

"You'll do nothing of the sort!" Francis shouted. I started, and Sara's head shot up from her hands to view her husband.

"I'm her guardian until the court makes their final decision, and Gemma is staying far away from you and that man of yours for now..."

I groaned. "He not 'my man', Uncle Francis. And I'm not happy about it either. I only want what's best for Gemma."

"It's best for her here!" Francis bellowed.

I stepped back from him, pressing my back against the wood-paneled wall behind me. I thought about the body in the barrel, the face that looked eerily like Patricia's daughter in the photo—Tanya. *This man could very well be a murderer. What if he murders me too?*

"Get the fuck out."

"Excuse me?" I'd heard him loud and clear, but maybe I just needed to hear it again.

"Get the fuck out!" Francis screamed, leaping up from the table, his chair banging into the wall behind him. This time, I listened, turning away from the dining room, starting for the front door. I would drive to Merrill's, steal my daughter away and skip town if I had to...

"No!"

Frozen mid-step, I turned around to see Aunt Sara on

her feet. "She's not going anywhere. She's my niece. You go, Francis! Get out of the house or go to our room. Anywhere but here!" She pointed toward the door.

Momentarily stunned, Francis stumbled back, hand over his chest.

"Where am I supposed to go, Sara? This is my house, too."

"Go take a walk. Have a drink; I don't care. Just cool off for a while," she said.

I bit my lip, watching Francis carefully. My fingers traced the outline of my phone in my jacket. He didn't know I had one, but I could yank it out and dial 911 quickly if I had to.

I waited for his reaction. Waited for him to scream and shout. To backhand timid Sara. But Francis did none of those things.

"I'm sorry, Sara! I'm just so upset over Gemma…"

Sara held up her hand, tight-lipped.

"I'll take a nap, okay?" Francis said.

I pressed my back to the wall as he brushed past me, holding my breath, then I flinched as the bedroom door slammed shut behind him. *What the hell just happened? Did Sara finally stand up to this creep?*

"Sara?"

My aunt was sobbing, face down in her hands. I didn't know what I should do.

"I'm sorry," I said, again, taking a few steps closer.

When she looked up at me, she looked beaten—cheeks red and eyes swollen with tears. I hated the way she looked like my mother. And I hated myself for feeling bad for her.

"I'm sorry you had to see that, Norah. I know that we all want what's best for Gemma. You're her mother, and who could blame you?"

Her words were shocking but soothing all the same. *So, it is Francis pulling the strings here then*, I thought, bitterly.

"I know about what happened with Constance. Connie. And I'm sorry."

Sara's eyes narrowed into slits. *That was the wrong thing to say*, I realized. I tried to correct it: "I can't imagine what that must have been like… how you all must have felt when her mother took her away and you never saw her again…"

"I think I'll go pick up Gemma from Merrill's now. You can talk to her about her father when we get back," Sara said, evading any mention of the young girl she'd taken under her wing previously.

It broke my heart, seeing her like that. Unable to even talk about it.

Sara stood and came around the table, placing her hands on my shoulders. "You are my niece. You are my blood. And you will always have a place here with me, any time you want it. Francis cannot make you leave this house. You only want what's best for your daughter, I see that now."

"Thank you, Aunt Sara. That means more than you know," I said, tearfully.

I watched her, shuffling slowly down the hall, as though she'd aged ten years over an afternoon.

Chapter Thirty-Six

I thought I would be unable to nap, with the concerns for Gemma so fresh in my mind, and the anticipation of her return. Talking to her about Allen wouldn't be easy, but it was a necessary conversation.

I'd been trying to focus on the *Big Book*, although what I'd really been doing was waiting to hear Francis downstairs moving around. It had shocked me earlier, seeing his submissive reaction to Sara. But, again, my mind wandered back to those pictures in the basement... Perhaps she was the only one he listened to, the only one who could get through to him.

Sara had been gone for nearly an hour, but she had mentioned needing to pick up some groceries and other items on her way to get Gemma.

Despite my worries, my limbs were growing heavy with sleep. The sun outside my bedroom window had disappeared, nightfall setting in. Each evening, I took my nighttime mental health meds at seven on the dot, and they usually kicked in and started making me sleepy at this time. Tonight, whether it was from the stress of the day or something else, they were causing me to feel extremely drowsy.

I made sure my room was locked and struggled to set my alarm for an hour, my eyes crossing and growing heavy with sleep.

I turned out the light, checked to make sure the door was locked again, and crawled into bed. Lying on my side, I read through my messages from Jana and Patricia. They were both worried about me, which was understandable.

The last thing I'd expected to find in this town was a friend, much less two of them.

I rolled onto my side, dozing instantly. But then my phone chimed, and I blinked, struggling to keep my eyes open. It was a text from Jana.

So, what's the plan for tomorrow? Want to meet up when I get done counseling at noon, have lunch and hit a meeting together? Might help to get your mind off things.

Jana was such a good friend. She had helped out so much since coming to town and I hoped that someday soon, I could return the favor—doing as much for her as she had done for me.

Sara volunteers at the school tomorrow and Francis works.
Maybe you can come here so we can talk? I don't want to leave
Gemma alone with them. She's coming back from Merrill's
tonight. She has school tomorrow but I don't want to leave her or
leave this house until I find out what's happening next…

I tried to type more, but my eyes were too heavy. I kept
nodding off, fingers fumbling in the dark. Finally, I flipped
my phone onto vibrate and tucked the covers up to my
chin. An hour nap was all I needed.

When my eyes flew open, I squinted through the darkness,
wondering what had woken me. I'd fallen asleep on my
phone, cheek pressed to the flip screen. It was the middle of
the night. Felt like 3 a.m. in my bones.

I couldn't see anything, just the shadowy lines and
edges of the bedroom furniture. I'd fallen asleep at seven
and never once heard my alarm. When did Gemma get
home? How long had I been out? Why did I get so sleepy,
and so quickly?

I sat up and opened my phone, blinked at two missed
messages. One from Patricia and one from Jana.

Patricia: *I'd like to come over tomorrow afternoon and help out.*
Jana said you're working on what you want to say to Gemma
about her father. I also found a list of some recommended

sponsors near where you're going. My point is... I'm here for you.

I scrolled down to Jana's message. I read it, then reread it a couple more times.

Jana: *What are you talking about? Sara doesn't volunteer at the school. She retired from there years ago before I started teaching and as far as I know, she has never volunteered there. Why would she tell you that? That's really odd, Norah.*

Huh? What the hell does that mean? I wondered.

If Sara wasn't volunteering at the school during her volunteer days, then where was she?

Has she been here, at the house, all along?

My spidey senses were tingling, the hair on the back of my arms raising on end, and not just because of Jana's message.

There was a sound, the real culprit that woke me. *Sturdy footsteps overhead.*

I pushed the covers aside. Held my breath. *My door is locked, so it's not like anyone's coming in... I'm okay I'm okay I'm okay.*

But my head was spinning still, too heavy for my neck. Why do I feel so tired and out of sorts? I fumbled for the light on the nightstand, reaching for my bottles of pills. My vision was narrowed and gritty from sleep, but I instantly realized that something was wrong. The tiny white pills that I took every night were different, tinged with blue. How in the hell did I miss that? And who fucking messed with my meds?

But then I heard an unmistakable creak and the scrape of wood on wood. It was a sound I recognized. Someone was coming through the hidden door in the playroom across the hall. Someone was sneaking straight toward my room.

Chapter Thirty-Seven

I was stock-still, waiting. My body stiff with fear.

After the bookshelf moved, there was silence for several seconds. As though whoever I was listening for was also listening for me. *Making sure I'm asleep.*

Then they were moving—the soft steady thump of feet moving across the playroom and crossing the hall to my room.

I held in a gasp as the shadow of two feet appeared below the bedroom door. I flipped the bedside lamp off. *So stupid! Of course, he probably saw the light flicker out!*

The door is locked; no one can get in. Can they?

I looked around me, searching for some sort of weapon. *If Francis thinks he can come in here and hurt me, he's got another think coming. And where is Gemma...? Oh God. Did he drug me with those blue pills and then do something terrible to her and Sara when they returned to the house while I was out cold?*

I'll kill him with my bare hands if I must.

But all that bravery melted away as I heard the sounds of metal turning. I fumbled for my phone in the covers, pressing buttons frantically in the dark. I tried to send out a message but dropped the phone before I could manage it.

The door to my room creaked open, slowly.

Chapter Thirty-Eight

"Get out of bed."

Sara stood at the end of the bed. She was wearing something sleek and silky, some sort of strange pajama set that reached from her neck on down.

"W-why? Is something wrong, Aunt Sara? Where is Gemma? I'm sorry I fell asleep... My medicine..."

"Yes. Something is very wrong, Norah. Very wrong with you. And we're going to take a walk," she said.

"I'm not going anywhere. Not until I see Gemma."

Something glinted in the darkness—something silver in her hand. I looked her up and down, my eyes shifting into focus. She wasn't wearing sleek pajamas; she had on some sort of plastic suit.

What the hell is she planning to do to me?

Sara raised the pistol I'd seen glinting in the darkness. She pointed the barrel straight at me.

"This is the last time I'll say it. Get the fuck out of bed right now."

Chapter Thirty-Nine

Every part of my body wanted to belt out a scream, but I knew it wasn't a good idea—*there's no one around to hear me, and that would just piss off the lunatic with the gun.*

"What's going on, Sara? Did something happen with Francis? Let's sit down and talk." The voice coming out of my mouth was no longer my own.

She poked the center of my back with the pistol, pushing me ahead down the forest path.

I started to talk more, ask questions… but this time, she took away all hope when she said, "Shut the hell up or I'm going to blow your head off, bitch."

I clamped my mouth shut, letting her lead me with the gun all the way to that dreaded shed. My stomach roiled with nausea.

If I go in that shed, I'm going to die. I'll never walk out of there. I'm not going to let that happen.

Sara pointed the gun at me with one hand and opened the shed with the other.

"You're not putting me in a fucking barrel like you did with Tanya Belfry," I said, breaking my silence.

Sara froze, ever so briefly, then turned to me and smiled. "I did that girl a favor."

"You think she wanted to die? Are you crazy?"

"Not Tanya. That bitch deserved no favors. Her daughter, Willow. A sweet girl. Smart too. I wasn't going to let that evil bitch come back to town and ruin her life again. If I'd have known that Grandma Patricia was a drunk too, I'd have shot them both."

"Why? Tell me why," I said, daring to take a small step back from my aunt.

"Get inside and I'll show you." She flung open the door of the shed and waved the gun for me to come inside.

"It was you that day, out here watching. You saw me break into the shed and find the body. Did Francis help you move the barrel after I called for help?"

"Francis isn't in charge, Norah. He never was. Unlike you, I don't choose men over my own children."

Gemma's not your child, I wanted to say, but didn't.

"But he would have helped me if he'd been here. I never thought you were that stupid... that nosy and ungrateful... but I should have. I had to grab the dolly from the basement and wheel it out here and take the barrel down the hill and dump it over the hillside with the others. Luckily, our moonshine barrel was in there too. That was stupid, so stupid... but you always were a stupid girl."

"Even if you kill me, Allen will come looking for Gemma... and my lawyer and the judge are expecting me back in court in a couple days. You can't just get rid of me, Sara... You don't have to do this. It makes no sense!" I screamed, my shout echoing back in my face, uselessly.

"Oh, you're wrong about that, dear. With your shady track record, no one will be surprised when I tell them you skipped town with Gemma. I'll play the role of sulky aunt, and no one will know the difference. I'll keep her tucked away, where she'll be safe from low-lifes like you. And don't talk to me about Allen! He's never fought to be in her life before. She wouldn't recognize him on the street if she saw him! Do you really think he'd fight for her now if I told him you were gone? He would accept my story, and so would the judge. They'll go on their merry way, living their stupid meaningless lives...a nd I'll get to keep my Gemma." Sara opened her mouth, and a hoarse strangled laugh came barreling out.

She's probably right about Allen. He'll believe I've run off with her; he never chased me in the past and he won't start now. My Gemma... My teeth were clenched so tightly that I could feel the enamel cracking. *She's not your Gemma; she's mine.*

"Where is my fucking daughter, Sara?" I hissed.

"Gemma is fine. She's more than fine! While you were passed out on the sedatives I gave you, I brought her home and showed her to her new room. She'll have so much more room to play upstairs, and no piece of shit absent fathers or junkie mother to deal with."

I sucked in several craggy breaths and shook my head

back and forth, trying to get my senses straight. "The room. The same one you kept little Connie in. That's where you put her, didn't you?"

Sara lowered her weapon half an inch, the first flicker of surprise.

"That's right. I know about your sealed-off room up there. I found it. What happened to her, Sara? I spoke to Tim. He said that her mother came and took her... but that isn't what happened, is it? You kept her for yourself, sealed her off in that room. Tried to keep the fact that you still had her hidden. You probably killed her mother, too," I said.

Sara chuckled, low and mean. "Didn't have to. I just paid Connie's mother off. And it didn't take much either, would you believe that? She probably spent the money Francis and I gave her, shot in her veins in less than a month!"

"Okay, I get it! Connie's mother was a low-life piece of shit. But what about your neighbor Tim, huh? He was out of prison, trying to get his life straight... He thinks his ex-wife skipped town with his daughter!" My words were sluggish, coming out slower than I'd intended. For the first time it dawned on me—if Connie didn't leave town with her biological mother, and she wasn't here with my aunt and uncle anymore, then where was she?

"Tim didn't deserve her either. He was a drunk, too. She was better off here with us."

"Was. You said 'was'. What did you do to that little girl, Sara?"

The pistol shook in her hand, eyes slitted with menace.

"She shouldn't have tried to run away. We gave her a good life, but she had too much of her mother in her! Things will be different with Gemma. Gemma's my flesh and blood... I would never hurt her that way."

I shivered. "I bet you said that to Connie, too. So, you killed Connie and you killed Tanya Belfry? Where is Connie's body, huh? What did you do? Toss her in a barrel like a heap of trash? You evil, vile woman!"

The gun came barreling toward my head before I could raise my arms to block it. It connected with my temple, and I hit the ground, groaning.

"Get on your feet and walk toward the shed," Sara hissed.

There's no use. She's not going to change her mind. And, no matter what, I'm not going in that shed.

Shakily I got to my feet. Sara held the gun in one hand, tugging at the door of the shed with her other. "Let me in!" she shouted, finally, smacking one palm against the grain.

My mouth fell open in horror as the doors to the shed swung outward, and Francis emerged from within.

I have to do something now. I can't let them take me in there!

I lunged for Sara, but she was too fast. There was a pop and that's when I felt it, the bullet like a punch to my gut.

Stumbling back, I was shocked that I'd been hit. Blood bloomed from the middle of my shirt, but I couldn't feel it. *I'm dying and I can't even feel it.*

"It's time," Sara said, moving toward me. I could feel her hands on my shoulders, but I was sinking, going down to the ground.

"I got ya now. It'll be over soon," Francis whispered in my ear. "And I'm sorry, but I have to do this. I have no choice…" he said. The world around me shrunk, finally melting away completely.

I didn't know how much time had passed before I awakened. I gasped for air, trying to move my arms and legs, but they barely gave an inch. That's when I turned my head and saw the aluminum siding—the metal monster that had become my tomb.

I was inside one of Sara's barrels.

Chapter Forty

STEP 11: SPIRITUALITY

There are twelve steps in AA. Breaking them down into one-word descriptions isn't easy. But I know how I categorize them, and I know it by heart. They are: Honesty. Faith. Surrender. Soul Searching. Integrity. Acceptance. Humility. Willingness. Forgiveness. Maintenance. Spirituality. Community.

I never made it to step eleven, and I probably never will.

Spirituality—making contact with a higher power (whatever that means to you). *Discovering the plan that God has for my life.*

Bleeding out and suffocating in a barrel—God only knows which will happen first—can't be my plan. *It can't be.*

I wasn't raised on religion. But the thought of something bigger, something powerful out there… had always appealed to me. I *should have worked harder to reach this step*, I thought, fearfully.

I know I'm supposed to accept the things I cannot change, and all that other bullshit, but I don't want to die here. It's not death that scares me, it's leaving Gemma. *She needs me now. She needs her mother. The version of her mother that fights and doesn't give up...*

I started rocking my body, side to side and back and forth. I could feel no pain, my body drained of its life force, so I pummeled myself as hard as I could in the small, tight space I had, trying to knock the barrel over.

I let out a small gleeful cheer when the barrel tipped over. I was just about to keep going when it slammed over on its side, jarring every bone in my body. *I will roll myself miles if I have to... roll myself all the way to Gemma.*

But then darkness started seeping in, everything shrinking around me.

Nonononono...

I could hear her name with every heartbeat roaring in my ears. *Gemma. Gemma. Gemma.* And I could see her—the day she was born, fuzzy in my arms. The doctors were surprised how strong she was, lifting her head up off my chest to look me in the eyes.

But I wasn't—I knew she was special from the very moment I felt her wriggling around like a butterfly in my womb. Gemma, walking for the first time, her tiny arms stretching out for me, a look of pure delight on her face. And Gemma, the last time I saw her... those sleepy eyelids falling shut after our bedtime story.

I love you, Gemma. I love you more than life itself... my love for you; the miracle that is 'us', our family, that is my purpose in life… That is my version of spirituality.

I only wish I had realized it sooner.

Chapter Forty-One

When I opened my eyes, everything turned white. Hot, white, and blinding. It wasn't until I heard the melodic beeping sounds, the warbled voices around me, that I realized where I was. A hospital room. A hospital bed.

Not a fucking barrel, thank God.

"Gemma." It came out as a croak, and I winced at the searing raw pain in my throat. It felt like I'd swallowed a handful of broken glass.

A face rose over mine, blurry at first, but then it came into focus. *Jana.*

I tried to talk but she put up a hand to stop me. "Don't talk, Norah. Please don't talk. You have a tube going down your throat."

My eyes widened.

"It's okay. You're going to be okay. And Gemma's fine. She's out in the hallway with her father."

Her father. I never thought I'd be so happy to hear anyone call Allen Gemma's father.

I tried to talk, ask questions, but Jana shushed me.

"Just listen. I'm not sure how much you remember but you were shot. Sara put you in a barrel."

I tried to shake my head at her, but I couldn't. My neck and head were secured in place.

"We got your messages, Patricia and me. You must have tried to text us before it happened. It was unreadable, do you remember? Just a jumble of letters and numbers you pressed. I figured it was an accident. That you had fallen asleep while texting. But not Patricia—she was so worried. Thought something was wrong, or that maybe you had relapsed…"

Thinking of Patricia, persistently nosy and doggedly determined to keep me sober, made me smile. But then I thought about her daughter Tanya, rotting in one of those barrels on my aunt and uncle's property, at the bottom of a hillside. If she didn't know already, she would soon. And Tim, too—soon he would learn the true fate of his daughter Connie. Was it better for them to know the truth of what happened, or would they be happier never knowing, thinking Tanya and Connie were out there somewhere, living their lives?

"You're such a fighter, Norah. You beat the hell out of yourself, despite your wound, trying to get out of that barrel. It was the banging that drew us to the back of the property. I'm so glad we found you. We thought… we thought we'd lost you. We tackled that maniac. Patricia took her down like a star quarterback; I only wish you could have seen it. And Francis? We didn't even have to fight him. He crumpled like a little bitch, told us where they'd hidden Gemma and begged us not to call the cops… Gemma's okay now, I promise. You're both going to be okay…"

I tried to move my right arm; tried to touch my friend. Somehow, she knew exactly what I wanted. We weren't blood, but we were family. She reached for my hand and squeezed it, interlacing her fingers with mine.

"You're still here, Norah. Through everything, you made it," she said.

Chapter Forty-Two

STEP 12: COMMUNITY

Three Months Later

Aunt Sara was right about one thing. I didn't need to go back to Chicago. Didn't need to return to that same old apartment or walk the same streets I'd strolled with Finn. I wasn't the same woman that I was back then. In a way, I'd been reborn.

It was time for a fresh start with Gemma. She needed it as much as I did, if not more.

After Francis and Sara were arrested for the murder of Tanya Belfry and Constance Jones, and my attempted kidnapping and murder, the judge issued an order for Gemma's immediate return to my custody. The local woman who lied for them also came forward. She admitted to lying; Francis and Sara offered her a measly four hundred bucks to do it.

Connie's remains were unearthed from the garden she used to play in. She had been strangled by the same people who claimed to love her. But, at least, she was finally returned to her father.

We rented a house in Galena. It's a small place, but huge compared to our old apartment. It's not fancy but we have bookshelves. And, most importantly, we have each other.

Allen lives less than a couple hours away. He's been taking it slow with Gemma, coming to visit on the weekends. Taking her out for ice cream. She seems to enjoy his company, and that's all that matters to me.

Patricia held a small service for her daughter before I left town. It was beautiful; there weren't a lot of people there, but her entire AA group were the first to show up. And Willow came home to see her, at least for a little while.

Patricia has been a godsend to me, calling every day. She hooked me up with listings of all my local meetings and she plans to come visit soon.

Jana is coming too, although she plans to stay much longer. She accepted a teaching job in nearby Freeport and plans to move here permanently. I can't wait to have my best friend closer. I plan to finish my teaching certificate while I wait tables. I may not have a perfect track record, but I think I have something good to offer, and I want to work with kids like Jana does.

Gemma and I are attending therapy, separately and together. Slowly, we will rebuild our lives. And we are building our own little family, and network of friends, one day at a time.

One step at a time.

Acknowledgments

I am forever grateful to my editors—Jennie Rothwell, Charlotte Ledger, Nicola Doherty, and Tony Russell—for supporting my vision of this book and offering me priceless feedback that ultimately made the story stronger. Thank you for making me a better writer and for believing in me. Also, thank you to all of the staff at One More Chapter and HarperCollins for working tirelessly behind the scenes and in front of the scenes to get my books in the hands of readers all over the world.

Thank you to my brilliant literary agent, Katie Shea Boutillier, and Donald Maass Literary Agency, for working so hard to sell this project and others… and for supporting me from the very beginning of this whole wild journey. I can't believe we're on books 7 and 8 together, Katie! Hopefully, there will be many more books to come!

Thank you to "Bill W.", the author of the *AA Big Book*. I referenced my copy countless times during the writing of this book, as well as aa.org! Thank you for the lessons and the inspiration.

Thank you to my family for seeing who I am and loving me anyways. Family isn't always just blood—it's about who shows up when you need it most and stays during your darkest moments...

Thank you to YOU, dear reader, for taking a chance on my books and spending your precious time in Norah's world.

Read on for an extract from Whisper Island

It was the perfect escape
Until one by one they vanished...

For friends Riley, Sam, Mia and Scarlett, their trip to
Whisper Island, Alaska, was meant to be a once in a lifetime
adventure – just four young women, with everything to
live for...

But as soon as they arrive things start to go wrong. As the
dream trip quickly turns into a nightmare, suspicion is
high. Are they really alone on the island?

And as each of the girls reveals a dark secret of their own,
perhaps the killer is closer than they think...just a whisper
away...

Watch Me

T he backbone of every triumph is built on two simple words: *Watch me.*

Like when my parents said I'd never make it to graduation, I whispered those words: *Watch me.*

And from that day forward, I never got in trouble at school. Never made another bad mark in class. Not because I believed them, but because I wanted to prove them wrong.

I'll prove so many people wrong.

Watch me.

When college after college rejected me, and a school counselor suggested that I might consider a different track, I shouted the words "Watch me!" to an empty hall of lockers and doors.

There are many more examples.

But all that matters is NOW.

Six of us are going to the island. Only one of us will make it back.

That one of us will be ME.

From the back of my mind came a familiar, snarky voice: *if you do this, you'll never leave that island. You'll never make it home again.*

But that voice was wrong, and I hadn't had a "home" in years.

As I stared in the mirror, eyes like two gaping holes staring back at me, I didn't say the words this time.

I didn't need to.

They were seared in my brain, writing themselves, like the unseen stylus of an Etch'n'Sketch engraving the words, deep and thick, across my cerebrum.

They rattled like a mantra, growing louder and louder, until they beat like a metal drum.

My lips moved silently in the mirror.

Watch me. Watch me. Watch me.

Chapter One

HOW IT STARTED

Riley

S ome might say we went too far.

After all, our plan was born in the span of one drunken weekend. Settled over shots of tequila.

But if you had to credit *one* person—or blame them— then I guess that one person was me. Ultimately, I was the one obsessed with puzzles.

I didn't want to hang out with them in the first place; just the mere junction of words like "group" and "project" gave my introverted ass an ulcer. I avoided people in college, determined to get the work done and get back to my lonely apartment.

But then there was Scarlett. Everything changed after Scarlett.

She was my bridge to the others, extrovert to my

introvert. Follower of all things art and art-drama related, Scarlett had followed the same track as me since freshman year. We shared the same three courses on Tuesdays and an early Foundation studio lesson on Thursdays.

If not for her annoying charm and persistence, our friendship probably never would have gained traction. In fact, I *know* it wouldn't have, because there's no way I would have initiated one in the first place.

I'd always been a loner, having fewer friends than I could count on one hand.

When I went to college, I never expected that I'd make a friend, much less more than one of them. Certainly not friends as glamorous as Scarlett, Sammy, and Mia.

"Riley, right? With an *i* or a *y*?" asked the girl with the bright red hair and million-dollar smile. Her hair was twisted into galactic spirals around her freckled face. She wore fake lashes and blood-red lipstick that was often smudged on her straight white teeth. She had a nice smile; the sort of smile you see in toothpaste commercials.

"Riley with an *i*," I stammered, watching curiously as she plopped down in the seat beside me. Before I could get a word in edgewise, she launched into a noisy monologue about two influencers in the art world who were up in arms on Twitter.

When the girl named Scarlett—of course I knew her name before she told me; it was impossible not to know a person that loud—was done talking, she drew in a deep breath then asked: "So, whose side are you on? 'Cause this shit is important to me when choosing friends." She winked and smiled, something playful but serious behind that cutesy facade. Still, I got the sense that she meant it. I had no clue who these influencers were, and I didn't mess around on Twitter.

Scarlett had a big dimple on her left cheek which reminded me of my first, and only, friend in school. Her name was Sierra—"like the desert, not the singer"—and she'd treated me terribly. Just the thought of that bitch made me clench my jaw.

I cleared my throat, considering the five-minute soap opera Scarlett had dropped on my lap just then. There was obviously a correct answer here, but I wasn't sure what it was.

It was a dispute over plagiarism—one artist claiming another's work too closely resembled their own. *Nothing new in the art world.*

But both artists were clearly respected and well-known, according to Scarlett. I should know about this, but I didn't.

"Truthfully? I'd have to see both pieces to make a fair judgment," I said and shrugged.

When you don't know the answer, just tell the truth. That's an adage I've always lived by, and it usually works out. Not always, but often.

Scarlett's eyes widened. "Excuse me? You haven't actually seen *The Donovans* yet? Where the hell have you been, Rye?"

I wasn't a big fan of nicknames. But I found, coming

from her, "Rye" sounded kind of ... endearing. *Sierra never would have called me "Rye", that's for damn sure.*

"I'm not much on social media," I admitted. Another painful truth-bomb. "I used to have an online journal, but I kept it mostly private..."

Scarlett stared at me, bug-eyed and silent, like she was seeing me for the first time, an exotic animal at the boring old petting zoo.

"Wow. Just ... wow. You don't know what you're missing. The drama on social media alone is worth it, but the connections, Rye ... the connections are everything in this business. It's important to know who's who ... what's trending ... well, don't worry. I'll show you the pics after class so you can see what I'm talking about. I need to know whose side you're on and then I'll know if we can be friends." There it was again: the wink-y smile, making me instantly feel at ease. There was something about her I liked, even though we were nothing alike.

"Okay, sure," I said, laughing awkwardly. I couldn't help feeling embarrassed, always out of the loop and in the dark about all things current on the art scene. It wasn't the first time I'd heard the speech about "connections". Nowadays, my classmates were already building their online presence, some going so far as to sell digital services or be commissioned to do pieces already. But, for me, it was less about connecting and pursuing fame, and more about stroking a compulsion. I'd lived with obsession for decades.

I didn't do art because I wanted to; I did it because I *had* to.

When I tried to imagine my future after college, walking out of those doors with a diploma in Fine Arts, I couldn't see my art displayed on the walls of some fancy exhibition … *Maybe I'll teach.*

But the thought of standing in front of a classroom, even a small one, was terrifying.

No. That's not an option either.

"Hey, I hope I didn't hurt your feelings. I admire it. You're all about the art, glory be damned. Fuck what the powers that be are saying or doing…" Scarlett nudged me.

A flicker of a smile must have shown on my face.

"Yep. I was right about you," Scarlett teased. Before I could ask what she meant by that, she was inviting me to lunch.

Lunch, for me, usually involved grabbing a quick sandwich in the commons, then hiking the mile back to my car, where I would sit in the AC and scarf down my food, hurrying to start the trek back across campus to my last afternoon class. There was a cafeteria in the commons and an outdoor patio, but I never knew where to sit. I preferred eating alone in my car, anyway.

"Okay. I don't think I've ever seen you in the commons before, though," I said, skeptically.

Scarlett released a bellyful of laughter, loud and snort-worthy, catching the attention of classmates nearby. We were all waiting wearily for Mr. McDaniel to show up for class; he was often late, sometimes drunk, and he liked to keep us over while he finished his lesson, as though he had no concept of time.

"Nah, silly. Nobody eats in that shithole! There's this Irish pub downtown, a few blocks from campus, and Tuesdays are dollar beer days."

I thought about my next class, less than forty-five minutes after lunch. *Would I be able to make it back in time?* I hadn't missed a class all semester. But one thing that reassured me: Scarlett was in my next class. If she had to be back on time, then surely, she would make sure we both were.

So that's how it started.

Trailing behind her in the school parking garage, I was happy to climb in the passenger seat of her yellow Mini Cooper, Billie Eilish blaring all the way to the Irish pub, O'Malley's on 11th Street, nestled between a boarded-up bookstore and a hemp shop.

When Scarlett told the hostess that two more were coming, I couldn't hide my surprise and disappointment. As an introvert, it was hard enough connecting with one person, let alone three.

"Don't worry. Sammy and Mia are cool. You're going to love them, I promise," Scarlett said, as though she could sense the bubble of anxiety that lived under my skin. *It's always there, brewing and bubbling, waiting to be squeezed until it explodes from within.*

But in the end, Scarlett was right. Mia and Sammy were cool, and I was excited, in particular, to meet Mia.

After that day, afternoons at O'Malley's became a regular thing, even sometimes on our days off from classes. It was a tiny, claustrophobic space with slabs of wood for tables and the faint smell of beer and piss embedded in the mothball-colored carpet.

But it was less about the atmosphere and more about the company. These three women intrigued the hell out of me.

Mia, with her feathery black hair dipped in blue, her shapeless paint-stained tops, she wore the uniform of "artist" well. She was gorgeous, stunning even, with the type of beauty that seems reckless and easy. The kind that feels unfair.

Sammy was different. Neatly pressed, she often sported button-down shirts and starched khakis, never a hair out of a place in her neat brown bob. She wore thick black glasses. No makeup. Despite her lengthy school hours, she maintained the books for a popular smoke shop in town, and I could often smell the tangy aroma of nicotine on her hands. I still wasn't sure why she chose art instead of accounting. She liked numbers and she was the most organized of the group. Scarlett joked once that Sammy was our "Velma" of the group, which of course made her our "Daphne", seeing as she was the only redhead of the gang.

Mia and I had looked at each other then. "If they're Velma and Daphne, who's that make us?" she'd teased. We were both dark-headed, Mia and I, but unlike her with her natural, fuck-it-why-try beauty and strange blue stripes, I had to work hard just to look presentable with my thinning hair and ruddy complexion. The extra pounds I'd been carrying for months didn't help either. *The freshman fifteen*, they called it. More like the "freshman fifty" for me.

"I guess we're Scooby Doo and Shaggy, unless you want

to be Fred?" I had teased, surprising myself when I got a laugh out of her. *Hell, maybe I can do this friend thing after all.* Mia had a great laugh; she would tilt her head back and open her lips as wide as they would go, then laugh from her belly.

Mia had taken an instant liking to me, which pleased me more than I cared to admit.

It was silly, the way the four of us acted. Getting sloshed during the middle of a weekday, cracking jokes about cartoons that showed our age, and listening to Scarlett's latest online gossip as though it were gospel. She liked to joke that Tuesdays were "church": "Come listen to me speak now, children," she often joked, taking the pulpit behind a table in a corner booth, lining up rows of tequila and bottles of beer.

But it was fun. Hell, it was so fun that I didn't mind missing the occasional class or being late anymore. I enjoyed feeling part of the "gang", even if it was only during school hours.

Mia was a painter, and the second she had walked in the pub, on that first day, I recognized her. How could I not have put two and two together? Mia was THE Mia Ludlow. Daughter of Cristal Ludlow, the famous local sculptor and painter whose work was easily recognized all over the country, and even internationally. But it wasn't just her mother's legacy that made me recognize her: no, Mia's work stood for itself. She had been spotlighted many times all over campus, and in some local papers as well. She was already well regarded in the art world because of her mother, but the work itself justified the attention. *Destined to outdo her mother*, one headline had read, featuring a nightmarish portrait of Jesus she had made on lithograph paper.

But according to Scarlett, there was more to Mia than met the eye. More than the talent and the famous name— she had a reputation. Everyone knew that scandal followed the rich girl, but nobody seemed to care.

Sammy and Mia, despite looking and acting like polar opposites, had been friends since grade school, growing up in Cement Ville together and competing against one another in local art contests and fairs. Now, they were no longer rivals, but best friends and roommates, they liked to proclaim.

Sammy liked to keep Mia's humility in check. "Oh, get over yourself, Mia," she often teased, rolling her eyes and smirking as Mia shared photos of her current works in progress, a dilapidated version of Monroe Institute, our school. It resembled the campus, buildings and landmarks easily recognizable, but everything was lopsided and distorted, the upside-down, creepy version of real life. And it was done in dark gray acrylic paint.

Mia had this style beyond compare; she took normal everyday objects and destinations and turned them into hideous versions of themselves. For me, viewing her art was like seeing my own soul on display, although I'd never admit that to her.

When you live with anxiety and depression, it alters the view on everything. Looking at her work made me feel seen; there's no other way to explain it.

All her work was hauntingly beautiful and a little disorganized, like Mia herself.

"Mia's a genius," Scarlett explained that first day (although I already knew that, as I'd been following her work on campus and in the papers for years). "We love her, but she's always in her own head, working through next steps, planning her next project... We like to keep her in the present, and of course keep her humble." Scarlett winked across the table at Sammy. We all knew Mia had gotten into some trouble her freshman year of college and she'd had to come back and do her freshman hours all over again ... but we never talked about that. I waited for the others to bring it up, but they never did. Her talent and legacy overshadowed any of the hidden parts of herself...

All three were different, yet there was something about each of them... Mia's careless beauty and dark genius. Sammy's snarky jokes and studious, know-it-all attitude. And of course, Scarlett, with her gossip and winky smiles. The girls didn't kiss each other's asses, but I could tell they were close; teasing often, but in a way that you knew meant love.

I couldn't help wanting a small piece of that for myself.

By the time our sandwiches and beers showed up that day, it was half past noon. Still nervous about the time, I drank my beer too quickly, feeling loose in the lips and warm to the touch within minutes of receiving my meal.

"There's no way we'll get back on time," I told Scarlett. *Is that a slight slur in my voice?* I had wondered, cringing.

"No worries, Rye. We'll just have a couple more, then finish our food. We'll be twenty minutes late, tops, I promise. And, hey, what does Grossman care anyway? It's not like he takes roll. Plus, it's college. We pay for these stupid classes. We shouldn't have to go to every single one if we don't want to," Scarlett said.

"Huh. I never thought of it like that," I burped, slugging down another beer. It tasted awful and flat, lukewarm on my tongue, but at that point, I didn't care.

As usual, Scarlett was right. Grossman didn't notice when we snuck in late that day, or any other day after. She flirted with him, batting those hideous, spidery lashes, and he always let us slide. I quickly learned that Scarlett didn't follow rules—as fun as she seemed, she was also impulsive. A few days into our friendship, I found her in the bathroom on campus, crushing up a pill with a razor. She snorted the entire thing in one fell swoop, then offered to chop me a line.

I shook my head and said, "No, thank you."

As the weeks went on, our Tuesday lunches turned into a regular thing. I stopped worrying about being late and started worrying about my friends. It's not that I was lonely or desperate for friends, the opposite, actually. The degree with which these women intrigued me was baffling, even to me.

Mia wasn't the only genius in the group. Over time, I learned more about Sammy and Scarlett's passions as well.

Sammy had a knack for computers and graphic design, creating some of the most incredible images; you'd never know they weren't sketched by hand. And Scarlett, for all her talk of gossip and scandal, and her small drug problems, had quite the impressive social media following. I didn't sign up for Instagram, but I googled her. Nearly 50k followers, and she posted day and night. Discussing technique and the latest trends in the art world; she always had something to say that drew people in. Did she create her own art, or spend all her time talking about it? I often wondered if it mattered anymore. She had a way with people—a skill so foreign to me, I'd prefer to recreate the Sistine Chapel than try to imitate Scarlett's presence online.

Weeks became months, and somehow, the friendships continued until the end of the semester, much to my surprise and delight.

I'm not sure how our hangouts evolved from weekly lunch sessions into weekend sleepovers... Well, that's not true. *I do.*

Again, it started with me. My suggestion.

"Tomorrow is Friday, y'all. Got any big plans?" Scarlett had asked one Thursday afternoon. We were piled into our normal booth in the back of the pub. The table was dirty, elbows sticking to the plastic placemats. Sammy, as usual, set to work, using her own pack of disinfectant wipes to clean off her space.

Scarlett nudged me, hard, in the ribs. "What are you doing this weekend, Rye?"

I tried to imagine how Scarlett spent her weekends. Images of that straw in her hand, residue fringing her nostrils, came to mind. I shrugged.

For them, weekends probably meant freedom and fun. For me, they were lonely. I looked forward to weekdays because I got to attend classes and see them, although admitting that seemed rather loser-ish now.

"Probably going to finish my puzzle," I said, finally. Normally, I wouldn't have brought up my puzzle craze, but I was tired, and too depressed about the impending weekend to care.

I expected them to laugh at me. After all, who spends their time doing puzzles? *Little old ladies, that's who*, I could imagine my old friend Sierra saying.

"Oh, damn. I love puzzles. I haven't done one in, like, I don't know … a decade," Mia exclaimed.

"Me neither," Sammy chimed in as she smudged the disinfectant wipe in a slow, methodical circle. "I like doing them online sometimes. Have you guys tried that puzzle photo app? You can take any of your photos and turn them into puzzles, then work them online…"

"Nah. I'd rather do a real puzzle. And a hard one too, like ten thousand pieces," Scarlett said, signaling for our waiter to bring another round of shots.

"You all should come over to my place. We could do a puzzle together," I said, an edge of hopefulness in my tone. It was like someone else talking, the words not my own. *Did I really just invite these girls over to my place—my tiny apartment with no working windows and few personal effects—to do puzzles together?*

I'd imagined inviting Mia over a thousand times, and the others too, but never this soon. And not like this.

"Hell yeah. I'm down. How about tomorrow?" Scarlett suggested.

Chapter Two

Mia

When the girl said she liked doing puzzles, that was a serious understatement.

Riley's apartment was a little weird, I must admit, small and cavernous—she had explained the windows were incredibly old, the kind you have to twist a crank to get open. Unfortunately, none of the cranks were working and she said they were too expensive to fix. Plus, it was hot, with very little air coming in or out.

I couldn't imagine living in that tomb, honestly.

No natural sunlight or fresh air. Yikes.

How does she ever get any sun? I couldn't help wondering.

Despite the lack of space, the apartment was neat and orderly, only a few personal touches on the walls. But I had to say, I felt a glimmer of pride when I saw one of my mother's sculptures placed delicately on her desk. It was a small one, probably the only kind she could afford, a woman with a buddha-ish belly and grotesque face. Mama's signature style—ugly and pretty at the same time. *Wonder where I get it from.*

When Riley saw me looking at the sculpture, her face burned red with embarrassment. I wasn't sure why she felt ashamed, most people like my mother's work.

But, back to the puzzles.

When Riley said she liked doing puzzles, she forgot to mention that she also likes to *make* them. She had a large steel die-cutting machine and thousands of corrugated cardboard sheets and molds for making her own designs.

For the first time, I realized: *we never once asked Riley about her art.* She was always quiet as a mouse, timid even, often listening instead of contributing during our weekly lunch sessions. We all had our own things; for me, it was painting, obviously. Sammy had her whole digital and graphic design thing, and Scarlett ... well, Scarlett was Scarlett, putting a face to the art, and all that.

Riley's puzzle-making equipment took up her entire bedroom, and since the tiny 600-square-foot apartment housed *only* one bedroom, I couldn't help wondering where the girl slept. There wasn't a bed in sight.

Does she even sleep? I wondered, looking around at all the completed and half-done puzzles lying around on the floor. For the first time, I noticed how pale she was, purple half-moons shading her eyes, zombie-like. *But the puzzles are freaking brilliant.*

"So, I have an idea. Hear me out." Riley was usually

quiet, but not tonight. Something lit from within as she stood by her shiny machine, stroking the steel like a prized family pet.

I liked her more than I ever had in that moment. That night, I saw something behind her eyes ... something that reflected my own. *Passion. The kind that gets down deep in your bones and leads to obsession.*

"Okay ... should we be scared?" Scarlett said. She looked distracted and slightly disgusted by the paltry apartment. In her arms, she was still carrying those cases of Corona with a bottle of Patron on top, and her pupils were tiny little pinpricks. She thought we didn't know about the drugs, but it was obvious to everyone who knew her.

"Yeah. Are you going to hack us up in your machine? Turn us into fleshy meat puzzles?" Sammy joked. She was poking at an all-black puzzle, nose scrunched.

I narrowed my eyes at my roommate. *That girl isn't right in the head. I love Sammy, but her sense of humor is a little off, most people missing her punchlines completely.*

"Ha! No, nothing like that," Riley said, strangely serious. "I was thinking we could come up with our own design together and then I'll make it into a puzzle. Afterwards, we can put it together. I might not have much room in here, but I do have a big kitchen table we can work at. Much better to put a puzzle together when you build it yourself..." She was rambling, obviously nervous.

"Whoa. That sounds fucking awesome," Scarlett said.

Riley's mouth spread into the biggest grin I'd ever seen.

I nodded. "Definitely."

Riley looked to Sammy last. She was always the skeptic, so I could see why Riley felt the need for her approval. As Sammy's roommate and oldest friend, I often caught myself tiptoeing around her, trying to keep her pleased, as well. On nights when she was working at the smoke shop, I felt more relaxed, more myself in the apartment alone.

Sammy shrugged. "Sure. I'm in. But I was thinking—".

"No. Don't you go trying to micro-manage this, Sammy," I warned, giving her a playful shove.

"No, no. Seriously. I'm not going to do that. I was just thinking … what if we used your design, Mia? The creepy painting of Monroe. Your painting, my digital skills, and Riley doing her thing on that crazy-ass chopping machine… How cool would that be?" Sammy suggested. There was something in the way she said it, something fiery behind the eyes. *Maybe we all have a little fire in us.*

I couldn't help feeling a little surprised that she wanted to use my Monroe design though. *Sammy loves me, I know that. But there's always this line between us, a thin veil separating friendship from competition.*

We grew up in the same town with the same friends … and for most of it, Sammy resented my popularity, but more than that, she resented my art. More than anything, I think she resented my advantage when it came time to apply for Monroe. I got a full ride—some would say it was because of my mom, but I liked to think I did it all on my own. And even after I got kicked out in freshman year, they let me come back. *Maybe it's a mixture. I can't deny I'm privileged; hell, I grew up with Cristal Ludlow as a mother.*

Chapter Two

When *Monroe—Another View*, my painting, was displayed on campus and featured in several prominent magazines, Sammy barely batted an eye. It's not that she didn't notice; I think she was jealous. She only mentioned the painting a couple times; it was a sore spot for her, I think. Hearing her suggest it as our puzzle design now gave me hope that all those hard feelings of the past had finally slipped away...

"Sounds good to me. Or, you know, we could use one of your own original graphic designs instead, Sammy," I offered.

"No way. We should do yours. It's the best. What do you two think?" Sammy turned to look at Scarlett and Riley.

Scarlett shrugged. "Fine by me."

Riley was grinning ear to ear, cheeks blossoming with pleasure. I was relieved to see a little color on her translucent skin. "I would love that," she said, gleefully.

So, that's how it started.

I guess if someone were to blame for Alaska and all that transpired there, it was me. After all, it was my design on the puzzle that started this rocky little friendship of doom.

Chapter Three

Scarlett

Let's be real: I'm the least talented one in the group.

It's no secret, really. And honestly, I don't give a damn. But ... that first night at Riley's apartment, I'd never felt more certain of it than I did right then: I was the odd one out of the four of us.

I didn't even know Riley made puzzles. I should have, considering I was the first one to make friends with the girl. Frankly, I was impressed. I didn't know how she could afford that equipment—*hell, where did the girl even sleep?*

Riley was painfully shy and withdrawn when I met her, but because of me, she was starting to come out of her shell. On that first day when I approached her in class, inviting her to join us for lunch, I was more than a little high, and more friendly than usual. I don't know why I befriended her. Maybe I was a little bored...

Truth is, though, I liked her. Riley was quiet and thoughtful, balancing out my boisterous side.

But with Mia's God-given painting abilities and Sammy's graphic art skills ... and Riley's woodworking genius ... where did that leave me in this equation?

Well, I'll tell you where—at the dead center, pulling the strings, as usual.

Because, the truth is, none of this ever would have lifted off the ground if it weren't for me.

When the design was done, I was the one who took the pictures. I was the one who presented the first finished puzzle to all of my fans online.

Because of me it went viral.

So, that's how it started.

I made a simple post—*look what me and my friends made!*

I added the proper hashtags of course, hoping for at least a thousand likes. Then we woke up to 300k likes and dozens of requests: *Where can I get one? How much? What's your Venmo? Do you do custom designs?*

The girls were humbled by the attention, but they didn't quite understand it.

Fame is a gift. You use it or lose it.

I pressured them. "We need to use this rise in popularity to our advantage. Feature ourselves all over the place online, force everyone to pay attention while we have them at our fingertips..."

"We should celebrate first ... take a trip together," Riley suggested, shocking the hell out of me. She was always the quiet one, but I liked her more in that moment.

"We could focus on our art. I could make more puzzles for Scarlett to post... We could even join some of our designs and make plans on our little girls' retreat."

Sammy was the first to say no. She had work to consider, and she didn't want to leave her brother Rob even for a short trip.

Mia said, "I don't know..." but she didn't really offer any good reasons not to.

I loved the idea of a girls' trip, a chance to bond and work on our art. A chance to celebrate the end of summer. But mostly, I needed to get away from my own self ... my own bad habits. If I ever wanted to be as talented as the other girls, I had to get my shit together.

It wasn't easy to change their minds. But influencing was *my* role.

I knew they'd come around sooner or later.

Chapter Four

Sammy

I might be the Debbie Downer of the group, but in truth, I'm the only one with sense, sometimes.

If there was one person who got this thing off the ground and kept it from floating away in the clouds ... well, that was me. I was the one who got us the house in Alaska for the summer. And I even found it for free. Well, it was my brother that mentioned it ... and it couldn't have come at a better time.

The idea of taking a girls' trip to focus on our art and celebrate our recent viral trip was a good one, but normally, I would have said no. Unlike the others, with their trust funds and scholarships, I had student loans out the wazoo. That's why I worked full time, barely sleeping as I ran back and forth between the smoke shop and class. But everything had changed now. School had come to an end, my future

315

plans in limbo, and with issues at my current job, I didn't have that to rely on anymore either.

The availability of an exclusive island in Alaska couldn't have come at a better time.

I know numbers and maps, exactly what it will take—money and time-wise—to get there. Plus, I was the only one who didn't waste my time drinking and gabbing and working on frivolous paintings all day. They needed me to organize the trip, or else it would have just been a pipe dream, something we talked about while we were drunk and making puzzles.

They needed someone level-headed in charge. They needed *me*.

"What's the matter, Riley?" I asked, trying to hide my annoyance. She was too quiet, too timid. Something about that bothered the hell out of me.

"I'm fine, I promise," Riley said, but she obviously wasn't fine.

"Spit it out. What are you anxious about?"

"It's the whole Alaska thing," Riley said, eyes lifting to meet mine.

"What's wrong with Alaska?" I asked, pacing back and forth on the worn carpet in front of where the girls were curled up on mine and Mia's sofa.

Scarlett looked away guiltily, sipping on a full glass of Jägermeister.

"You too?" I asked, pointedly.

"It's just … I'm not fond of Alaska either," Scarlett admitted, slamming back the rest of the drink then wiping her mouth with a long black sleeve. "Isn't it cold there all the time? And dark half the time? Fuck that, Sammy. If we're going somewhere remote to focus on our art, can it at least be warm and tropical?"

"I'm a nervous flyer..." Riley blurted out, sheepishly.

Why does that not surprise me? I gave Mia a look that said, "Can you believe this girl?' but she looked away, patting Riley on the shoulder like a baby kitten.

"Yes, Scarlett, there *are* places in Alaska that go dark for long periods of time. It's because of the way the Earth is tilted... Well, never mind. The important thing here is that most of the state does not go dark, and even those parts that do are for only thirty to sixty days. It won't affect us where we're going. Also, Alaska isn't cold in the summer. It's like eighty degrees in some places!" I said.

Scarlett tilted her head side to side, considering, then reached for another drink.

"And as far as flying, Riley, we can get you a sedative. One of my foster dads used to be terrified of planes, but then the doctor gave him something to take for the flight on the way to Nevada. He slept like a baby the whole way there. Fear of flying is something you need to get over, anyway."

Riley nodded, but still, I could tell she wasn't on board.

"I don't get it. Why Alaska? We could go anywhere..." Mia started.

I felt a flash of annoyance. Mia was my best friend, but until the others had showed up to discuss this, she'd made no mention about any doubts. *She's supposed to be on my side.*

"Alaska wouldn't have been my first choice either," I sighed. "But after our talks the other night about focusing on our art, I figured this was the first place to disconnect. No one can reach us there. And my brother found it. It will be completely free for three whole months; all we have to do is pay for our flights and a boat ride to the island."

"Your brother. Really, Sammy? What does he have to do with any of this?" Mia said, bitterly.

Mia and my brother Rob didn't get along. They'd dated for a while and it hadn't ended well. Since Mia and I are roommates, I usually don't feel comfortable inviting him over to the apartment we share. And even when he calls, Mia acts like her feelings are hurt. As though I must choose her or my brother. *Ridiculous.*

"He's the reason I came up with Alaska. His friend sent him a picture of this, said we could stay there rent-free for three months. I repeat: rent-fucking-free."

I took the map out of my back jeans pocket and unfolded it. I spread it across the coffee table in front of them for all to see.

"This," I pointed at the map, "is Whisper Island."

It was a hand-drawn map. And although Mia liked to think of herself as the "real artist' in the group, I'm a pretty good sketch artist myself.

"Okay," Mia said, squinting at it then looking back up at me, questioningly. "Are we hunting treasure or what?" she said, a ripple of laughter in her tone.

Ignoring her, I said, "The island is a thousand square miles, located near the tip of the Alaskan Peninsula. It is surrounded by the mysterious Bering Sea. It's one of the most beautiful places on earth."

The girls looked at each other, still unsure.

"And, like I said, we'd get to stay there for free for three months."

They still didn't look convinced. The cool map and the incomparable price tag—or lack thereof—clearly wasn't enough. *But I knew that before I brought it up. I couldn't tell them the truth—that going to a deserted island and getting the hell out of Tennessee was my best bet right now, with or without them.*

"Let me show you the real pictures of it," I said.

I crossed the room and retrieved my backpack. I'd printed out dozens of photos my brother had sent me online, using up every bit of high-resolution ink on my printer.

"This is Whisper Island," I repeated, dumping the glossy photos on the table in front of them.

I'm not sure which one of them gasped first, but I knew I had them then.

Whisper Island was breathtaking; an isolated strip of heaven with a miniature mansion and three workable outbuildings. *It's perfect for me*, I thought.

"All we would need is our plane tickets and we're on our way there…"

Of all the girls, Riley looked the most mesmerized, locking in on the photos. She held one up of the main house on the property, studying the shiny glass windows on the second floor as though she could see a tiny person inside.

"How soon can we go?" Riley asked, breathlessly.

So, that's how it started.

I took our little idea and simple plan and turned it into something real ... but also something magical.

"This will be quite the adventure," Scarlett said, smiling with all her teeth.

I hope so, I thought, cringing internally.

Don't forget to order your copy of *Whisper Island* to find out what happens next!

ONE MORE CHAPTER

One More Chapter is an award-winning global division of HarperCollins.

Sign up to our newsletter to get our latest eBook deals and stay up to date with our weekly Book Club!
<u>Subscribe here.</u>

Meet the team at
<u>www.onemorechapter.com</u>

Follow us!
𝕏 <u>@OneMoreChapter_</u>
f <u>@OneMoreChapter</u>
⧉ <u>@onemorechapterhc</u>

Do you write unputdownable fiction?
We love to hear from new voices.
Find out how to submit your novel at
<u>www.onemorechapter.com/submissions</u>